For
"Best Girl"

'Tis the good reader
that makes the good book.'

. . . Emerson

THE DISTRICT MAN

THE DISTRICT MAN

Peter Cook

JANUS PUBLISHING COMPANY
London, England

First published in Great Britain 1996
by Janus Publishing Company,
Edinburgh House, 19 Nassau Street,
London WIN 7RE

Copyright © Peter Cook 1996

**British Library Cataloguing-in-Publication Data.
A catalogue record for this book is available from the
British Library.**

ISBN 1 85756 296 8

Cover design Harold King

Printed & bound in England by
Antony Rowe Ltd,
Chippenham, Wiltshire

Contents

Deadly Rivals   1
The Vicar and the Wife-swappers   26
Sudden Departure   42
Hive of Political Intrigue   68
The Law Truly is an Ass   80
Flight of Fancy   101
Lilies at a Funeral   120

Deadly Rivals

North Yorkshire c1970

Shirley Passman, the editor's busy secretary, was normally a warm friendly woman, but today she was obviously ill at ease. She jumped nervously as I entered her office, and without a word she crossed quickly to the adjoining office from where I could hear Paul Winter on the telephone. Putting her head round the door she whispered, 'Mark is here.'

I heard him briefly halt his conversation and say, 'OK, give me two minutes.'

'He won't be long,' she said softly, returning to her desk.

Then she smiled bleakly, I knew I had problems.

It was no secret that the *Clarion* was losing money and that circulation was still falling. The trouble had begun twelve months ago with the devastating announcement that the Steel Works in Burnthorpe was to close. You didn't have to be a financial wizard to forecast the effect mass unemployment would have on the local economy, and many businesses in the high street had already bitten the dust. The shock waves had quickly rippled through the advertising and circulation departments of the *Clarion* and its sister paper the *Weekly Times* where revenues were now at an alarming all-time low.

With two freesheets and the opening of a new commercial radio station all thrusting for a slice of the diminishing revenue cake, the situation was critical. Yet against the odds Paul Winter was doing a good job. Under his stewardship the *Clarion* recently had won two major editorial awards. But as they say, trophies don't pay bills, and everyone knew he was under intense pressure to cut costs.

He and I had been friends from the day we both joined the paper as trainee reporters ten years ago. When later I was lured to Fleet Street, Paul had remained loyal to the *Clarion* and it came as no surprise when finally he settled into the editor's chair.

My colleagues in London on the country's leading national tabloid had thought me raving mad when I had announced I was leaving to return to the provinces to work for my old mate. But my enthusiasm for the London life had waned, especially after a disastrous relationship with the picture editor's ex-wife. I had begun to yearn for my native Yorkshire and had taken no second bidding when Paul offered me a vacant sub-editor's chair at the *Clarion*.

Despite the drop in salary I knew I had made the right decision the moment I re-entered the large grey building in the centre of the market town of Ellerthorpe. I had felt relaxed. I was back home. Now, if I read the signs right, I was about to be made redundant.

I heard Paul replace his receiver and shout, 'OK Mark.'

He was looking edgy and depressed as I entered, and I decided to put him out of his misery.

'Look Paul, you don't have to dress it up,' I began.

His desk was covered with the daily confusion of news gathering. He beckoned me sit down on the hard wooden chair in front of it.

'I don't want to lose you, Mark,' he began apologetically, 'you know that. But my hands are tied, and to be fair I have to follow the last in, first out principle.'

He took off his glasses and wiped them vigorously with his pocket handkerchief, squinting at me all the while. 'The accountants are running things here as you know, but I have managed to screw some form of compromise from them. Not much, but it might help.' He replaced his glasses. 'Since Jim

McBain retired, our coverage in the surrounding countryside has been almost non-existent. Agreed?'

I nodded. McBain had been an excellent stringer, but I knew that because of the financial constraints Paul had been unable to replace him.

'Well, I've managed to make the men in grey suits see sense. If I'm going to rebuild circulation I need to generate stories from the districts. In short, I need a good district man.'

Interesting. Perhaps the future wasn't so bleak after all.

'There's a snag though – a big snag.'

Isn't there always, I thought.

'It's not a staff appointment – more a freelance contract. I can pay a small retainer and the *Weekly Times* will chip in with a similar amount, but the bulk of your earnings will come from the stories you file with us, providing they make the paper.'

'Expenses?'

'Nope.' He shook his head discouragingly. 'But we have no objection to you working for the nationals, provided you give me an equal bite of the cherry and you regularly cover the courts and council meetings for us.'

'It's not much of a deal, Paul.'

'It's the only one on the table, and it's more than I am offering the others.'

'I'm not the only one to go, then?'

He shook his head. 'Bill Stand, Hazel Berwick and Harry Gorton.'

I winced as he listed the other redundancies.

He leaned forward. 'Listen Mark, if anyone can make a go of freelancing, it's you. You're a good sub-editor but you're a *bloody* good reporter and with your contacts with the nationals you could make a bomb.'

I smiled sadly at his enthusiasm and wondered how many national stories had appeared recently from the villages and hamlets he was asking me to cover; the world with all its alarms and dramas had been passing them by for centuries and seemed set on continuing on the same path.

'Think about it. Let me have your decision by the end of the week.'

He handed me a brown envelope with my name typed on it. It was the first time in my career I had been asked to leave a job, and as I rose and stuffed my notice in my inside pocket, I felt hurt and angry. I wanted to storm and shout. Instead I nodded, and returned to my desk. Two weeks later my flat in Ellerthorpe was on the market and I was looking for digs in Sessington.

That was eighteen months ago and, looking back, it was the best thing that could have happened to me. At the outset I was consumed by a fear of failure. For the past two years I had enjoyed the security of a desk job at the *Clarion*, subbing and re-writing other journalists' copy, and before then I'd enjoyed a camaraderie and fellowship of the editorial team on a national newspaper responding to assignments from the news desk. Now I was on my own and I had to fight against a sense of abandonment. But my fears about the lack of good stories in this rural area were unfounded, and by milking my media contacts in London and Manchester I had quickly become an accredited stringer for the nationals. To start with I relied heavily on the retainers the *Clarion* and the *Times* were paying me, but once I found my feet, I began making serious money, so much so that nine months ago I took the plunge and obtained a mortgage on a small detached cottage in Bardsey, a village about three miles from Sessington.

Jill and I spent what free time we had renovating it. Jill Croydon is a nurse at Mallingborough General Hospital where I had been admitted with appendicitis shortly after leaving the *Clarion*. I had been quite captivated by this attractive girl in her late twenties and two weeks after my discharge, using the pretence of thanking her for looking after me, I rang her and had been delighted when she had accepted my invitation to dinner. I discovered she was separated, her husband having walked out on their second wedding anniversary to live with a wealthy widow twice his age. Over coffee she had made it clear that the last thing she was looking for was a complicated relationship, and on this understanding we agreed to see each other again. But during the months following, we both recognised a physical and emotional bond developing. The word marriage was never mentioned, but it hung permanently in the air nonetheless, and it was strong enough for us to take the decision to live together; and despite Jill's shift work and the erratic hours I keep, our romance continues to flourish.

The *Clarion* and the *Weekly Times* still required me to cover all the diary jobs for them, especially the parish council meetings. These local councils are a bit of a pain. They have very limited powers, and act more as watchdogs, forwarding complaints and suggestions to the larger and more powerful Bridgefield District Council. Sitting in on these meetings can be as stimulating as watching paint dry, but the *Times* prides itself in covering all local events, a policy that has actually increased circulation, and Paul Winter at the *Clarion*, in taking a leaf out of this book, is also actively chasing the rural reader. He is prepared to leave the parish pump stuff to his *Times* colleague on the floor below him, but he encourages me to search out good human interest stories from these parts.

A bum-numbing two hours was in prospect therefore when I ducked into the small 16th-century parish meeting room in Sessington. The village goes back to the 12th century and with its population of just over four thousand is one of the larger in this part of the country. Regular incursions from wealthy newcomers who buy up and modernise some of the old properties, have not diminished its original charm. At its heart is the river, flanked by a large green cropped by a resident flock of sheep. An attractive square accommodates half a dozen shops, library and parish meeting room and a couple of pubs.

I found Mrs Edith Perth the meeting room caretaker on her knees trying to induce more life into the open fire.

'There's not a grate in't village that'll burn reet with wind in the east,' she growled, grasping a chair and arthritically hauling herself upright. 'You'll just have to open yon window if the smoke gets to your bronichals.'

Edith Perth, had lived in the village of Sessington all her life. No one actually knew how old she was – 'that's for me to know and you to find out' she would tell those brave enough to ask – but she must have been well into her eighties. Invariably wearing a floral apron and her white hair scraped back into a large bun, she was a distinctive figure in the village. She lived alone in her cottage next to the church, fiercely independent, beholden to no one, yet always available to lend a hand to any good cause. Functions in the village hall were incomplete without Mrs P. helping with the supper and washing up afterwards. She arranged the flowers in the church, visited the sick and looked after the parish room and library which she kept spotless. A devout Christian, she took her place every Sunday at church, occupying the same pew for as long as anyone could remember. We had a good relationship, she was an avid reader of the *Times* and she was the kind of contact every district reporter needs to cultivate. There wasn't much that happened in Sessington that Mrs P. didn't know about.

Reginald Parks who now poked his head around the door and politely bade Mrs Perth and myself good evening, was another mine of information. He had been clerk to the parish council for fifteen years. Known affectionately as Old Parksie, he was a neat little man in his seventies with an impressive head of thick white hair, a retired bank manager, of the old school, who still dressed the part. I had never seen him at these meetings wearing anything other than immaculate pressed pinstriped trousers, a spotless white shirt with a dark tie, and a black jacket from which he now took a black Waterman fountain pen and propelling pencil and laid them neatly alongside his papers.

He hung his raincoat behind the door and meticulously began positioning five chairs so there would be two either side of him, and one at the end of the table facing him. Then placing copies of the agenda before each place setting, he opened the heavy minute book, each resolution painstakingly recorded in his well-ordered copperplate handwriting. Finally, to one side of the fireplace, he pulled up an old wicker chair which I could occupy as the only member of the press present. It was all done with such a sense of grooved habit and deliberation that you felt the world was secure with Parksie around. The other members of the council began to assemble. John Briggs, the chairman, a rotund jovial farmer and a true blue Tory on whom I could always rely for a good quote, arrived carrying a dozen eggs on a cardboard tray which he handed to Mrs Perth.

'What's these for?' she demanded.

'Your birthday present,' he beamed.

'It's not my birthday and you know it.' Her face was stern but her pale grey eyes shone. It was their standing joke, Briggs, a heavy man in his late sixties, brought her eggs every month, and at Christmas he always presented her with a turkey or goose, and his excuse was always the same, the celebration of her birthday, the date of which, like the rest of us, he hadn't a clue.

Before Mrs Perth could further protest at Briggs' generosity, the door opened and Ann Scrolls entered and immediately began coughing and screwing up her eyes.

'We'll have to do something about this wretched fire, we can't work in this atmosphere,' she said, moving purposefully to throw open the window.

The draught caused Mrs Perth's fire to discharge another large plume of grey smoke into the tiny room and scatter the papers which Parks had so neatly arranged on the table.

Briggs winked at me, and slowly shook his head and raised his eyes to the low oak beams. He and Ms Scrolls sat at opposite ends of the political spectrum, and seldom agreed on anything. She was a teacher at the comprehensive school in Bridgefield ten miles away and had arrived in Sessington about seven years ago with her teenage daughter. No one knew the whereabouts of Mr Scrolls; rumour had it that his drink problem had broken up their marriage. Ann Scrolls, an avowed feminist and a member of the socialist party, which meant that she and Briggs were always guaranteed to bring the worst out of each other. Not only was he a parish councillor, he was also a district and county councillor and this enhanced status only served to heighten their conflict.

Harry Jenkins and Sean Kelly arrived together. I liked Sean, a small untidy man with laughter lines around his eyes, who had retained his Irish sense of humour. He was an excellent mechanic, and I had been indebted to his garage in the centre of the village more than once for keeping my car on the road. Harry Jenkins on the other hand was not my type at all. An overweight sullen man in his late fifties, he owned the village butcher's shop and almost begrudged you the time of day. He despised the press, yet always took me to task if I hadn't mentioned his name in the council report.

As usual the last member to arrive was Fred Hopgood the local dairyman, an athletic man who captained the local cricket team. He, like Ann Scrolls who had scraped home in the last election three months ago by just six votes, was a relative newcomer to the council but the Hopgood family went back generations, and Fred's father and an uncle had both served as chairman of this council. Fred helped Mrs Perth struggle into her long tweed coat, she bade us all goodnight, wheezed her way into the autumn evening, closed the door behind her and John Briggs opened the meeting.

The agenda covered the usual crop of complaints about dog fouling, parking problems, a need to tidy up the river bank, inefficient street lighting. Hardly the stuff to stir Paul Winter at the *Clarion*. Briggs and Scrolls enjoyed their usual spat when she had suggested the village needed traffic lights at a rather tight junction in the high street, but she had been left isolated after Briggs had enjoyed telling her that such a suggestion had already been turned down by the county council nine months earlier.

'Before your time, councillor,' he'd added pointedly.

It was only when the meeting got to any other business,

normally the cue for raising a ragbag of uninteresting minutiae, that I perked up at the word bombs.

Parksie was reading out a letter he had received from a Mr Bert Tickett who after reading about a cache of explosives being found in a field in Sussex, had recalled cases of ammunition being buried at Badger's Cross, a stretch of land backing onto a row of cottages adjacent to the village green. According to his late father, who had been in the local wartime Home Guard, the area had been used as an ammunition dump in the early 1940s and to the best of his knowledge the ammunition had never been recovered. Was this a matter for the parish council, he wanted to know.

Things were looking up. I brought out my notebook again.

Mr Tickett had enclosed a rough map of where he considered the explosives were buried and Briggs replaced his half-moon spectacles and examined it closely.

'That's now old Pargeter's garden,' he announced finally. 'He's been working that plot for twenty years to my knowledge. If there was owt there he'd have been blown up long before now.'

Cllr. Kelly's boredom threshold was about to be breached, it was getting uncomfortably near closing time and he had a fiendish thirst. He pointedly looked at his watch and proposed the letter be sent to the police and after more discussion it was agreed to follow Sean's suggestion.

It had gone ten thirty by the time I arrived at Jim Pargeter's cottage and I wondered if he would still be up. I had met this tough little character once at an agricultural show when I interviewed him about his prize leeks and giant onions for which he was renowned. He was a former miner from County Durham who had moved to Sessington to live with his sister. She had died some years ago.

As I walked up the narrow path I could see a light shining behind the curtains and in the absence of a bell I knocked hard on the door. From behind a rose trellis, a window opened and a voice shouted,

'Who's there. What do you want?'

'Mark Devlin from the *Times*. Sorry to disturb you, Mr Pargeter, but it is important.'

The window slammed shut, and a few moments later the front door opened to reveal Jim standing in a dressing-gown tied at the waist with a trouser belt.

'It must be bloody important at this time of night,' he growled.

'It's about a letter to the council that affects you.'

'Oh aye.'

'I've just come from the meeting.'

'You'd best come in.'

I followed him down the badly lit passage into the back room. It was like entering a large potting shed, plants and cuttings were everywhere and it smelled like a greenhouse, on a warm day. A small propagator containing seedlings was perched on a pile of old newspapers and around the walls were certificates and rosettes bearing testimony to his fine show performances. He moved three seed trays from a rickety wooden chair for me to sit down, then unceremoniously throwing a mangy cat off an old arm chair, he sat opposite me next to the dying fire.

'Well? What's to do?'

He continued to chew on a piece of tobacco as I pulled out my notebook and read him the gist of Tickett's letter, adding, 'John Briggs reckons that Tickett is referring to the piece of land you bought to extend your garden just after you moved in here.'

'What of it?'

'If he's right,' I concluded, 'you could be sitting on an arsenal.'

'Bollocks.' He spat the word into the fire, causing the embers to hiss and the cat to seek safer refuge. 'If anyone comes rummaging in yon garden they'll find a garden fork up their arse, and that goes for Bert Tickett. *Especially* Bert Tickett. He'll do owt to scupper yon leeks.'

'Why would he want to do that?' I asked.

'Plain bloody jealousy, that's why. He's never beaten me yet in any class. He knows if yon land was dug over now I would have no chance at Bridgefield Show.'

Bridgefield was one of the biggest agricultural shows in the region and to win there was to stake a real claim to fame.

'You mean this bloke Tickett has raised this alarm deliberately to have your garden dug over to foil your chances?'

'Stands to reason.' He hoisted himself upright. 'Well, I won't be losing sleep over it. No one comes onto my land, and you can tell that to those bloody interfering councillors.' He poked me on the chest with a gnarled finger to further make his point.

'It might be too late,' I said. 'The police will be informed of Tickett's letter in the morning, and the chances are you'll have the army bomb disposal lads knocking on your door before breakfast.'

'Aye, and they'll be standing there long after supper an' all.'

As he closed the door behind me I knew that if Pargeter was right about Bert Tickett's motives, I was sitting on a national story, especially if the bomb disposal crew were involved and they were refused entry by the old man.

I knew nothing about Tickett, apart from hearing Briggs say he was a bus driver and lived on the council estate. It was too late to seek him out tonight, that would wait until morning, and there was no point in contacting the police for a statement until they had heard from the parish council.

Jill was in her dressing-gown brewing tea in the kitchen when I got in. She had just got out of the shower and she smelled warm and fragrant as I put my arms around her waist and kissed the back of her neck and felt her hair damp on my cheek.

'I thought you would be in bed before now.'

Smiling, she stifled a yawn. 'I was just going up. How was the meeting?'

I gave her the bare bones of the Pargeter story, but she had been on duty since seven that morning and just wanted to crash out.

'Will you be long?' she asked yawning.

'No, I'll just make the calls and then I'll be up.'

These regular calls to the police and fire brigades and ambulance services play an essential role in local news gathering and create a kind of journalist's Sod's Law. On a quiet news day when I'm scratching around for a story, the duty officers will have nothing to report. On the other hand if I'm battling against deadlines with a number of stories, you can bet all hell will be breaking loose outside, like one memorable occasion when, with only two hours to a midnight deadline, I was confronted with a major road crash, a house fire, and an attempted murder.

Fortunately, tonight was all quiet and within five minutes I crept into bed and slipped my arms around Jill. She was sound asleep and the next morning she had already left for the hospital before I was awake.

I spent the early part of it ringing around the national news desks selling the idea of the Pargeter story and discussing its treatment. Apart from the *Guardian*, always a bit sniffy about this type of story, the rest received it enthusiastically. I could have offered it exclusively to one tabloid, but I calculated that it would pay me to syndicate it. The local BBC and ITV stations were particularly keen and asked me to liaise with camera crews and reporters they were sending, and the local radio stations, always ravenous for news, welcomed me with open arms. Tom Hall the *Clarion*'s news editor was equally enthusiastic leaving me to organise pictures with Harry Gorton a former *Clarion* photographer who was now a fellow freelance.

My next call was to Supt. Bill Williams at Mallingborough, one of my better police contacts who confirmed that Reg Parks had already telephoned him about Tickett's letter.

'WPC Falls will try and have a word with Tickett and Jim Pargeter this morning and then we'll decide what to do.'

Sally Falls was the popular local beat officer, a young and

attractive woman, good on community relations who charmed her way around the village. If she couldn't make Pargeter see sense no one could.

'Are you alerting the army bomb squad?' I asked.

'No point, there's nothing for them to handle.'

I got the impression that Supt. Williams was not placing this incident very high on his priority list.

As I drove to Sessington to find Bert Tickett the countryside was shimmering under the warmth of the September sun and the hedgerows were draped in silver cobwebs still sparkling from the early morning dew, and I knew autumn must be just around the corner when I noticed two young lads rummaging around the foot of a huge horse chestnut tree in search of the burnished brown conkers. Either side of the twisting lanes farm workers busied themselves in the stubble fields loading trailers with bales of straw. This time of year always induced in me a strange feeling of warmth and anticipation, almost as if I was looking forward to winter wrapping its dark cloak around the countryside. Jill on the other hand hates the thought of winter and can't enjoy the fruitfulness of autumn for thinking about the prospect of cold, dark and depressing nights.

Approaching the top of Sessington Bank I stopped to admire the view. The air was crystal clear and I could even see the Pennine peaks forty miles away. A lone glider from the local flying club on top of the moor, banked and disappeared below the ridge. I never tire of this view, it makes me want to take a deep breath and it reinforces my decision to get out of London and a city existence. Reluctantly I slipped the car into first gear and began the hazardous one-in-three descent, my ears popping.

The small council estate in Sessington comprised eight semi-detached, grey pebble-dashed houses, located in a crescent close to the cemetery. A woman who was shepherding two small children across the road told me that the Ticketts lived in the end house and as I approached the front door I stopped to admire a superb display of chrysanthemums in the front garden, and in the side garden there was a healthy crop of leeks. I knocked on the door.

A forty-something woman answered wearing a short denim skirt and a tight mauve sweater beneath which a slack bosom responded to her every movement.

'Mrs Tickett?'

She dragged deeply on her cigarette, swaying slightly, then slowly, and quite deliberately, blew smoke and alcohol fumes into my face. Her reply was slurred.

'Depends if you're buying or selling.'

She watched the smoke disperse above my head with glazed eyes, and it didn't take a genius to conclude she had been hitting the bottle.

'I'm looking for Mr Tickett.'

She started a bleary examination of my toes, then slowly worked her way to my thinning fair hair and back again like a yo-yo.

'And you are?'

'Mark Devlin. I'm a reporter following up Mr Tickett's letter to the local council about explosives buried near Badger's Cross.'

Her eyes widened in mock astonishment.

'You do lead an exciting life.'

'Is he in?'

She stepped aside and invitingly opened the door wide. For a split second I hesitated before squeezing past the perfumed bosom and stepping into a room overlooking the back garden. There was no sign of Bert Tickett.

She flopped onto a well-worn settee crossing her legs and exposing a wide expanse of upper thigh.

'Do I take it Mr Tickett isn't at home?'

She tapped the settee cushion beside her. 'Come and tell me all about it.'

Ignoring the request, I sat at the cheap dining table covered by a badly stained cloth on which were a half empty gin bottle and a packet of cigarettes. She bent down and picked up her empty tumbler next to her feet and with an unsteady hand leaned across and handed it to me, nodding towards the bottle.

'How well does Bert know Jim Pargeter?' I asked, pouring gin into the glass.

'Hates his guts.' She blew a cloud of smoke at the ceiling.

'Why's that?'

'Can't better him, can he, can't better Lucky Jim. Knows his onions, does Lucky Jim.'

She stared silently at me, then without warning laughed drunkenly as she reached for her refilled glass.

'I don't suppose you have a photograph of Bert's father?' I asked.

She looked at me hard, then lurched over to a shelf next to the television and picked up a photograph of two men standing next to a motor cycle and tapped her finger at the smaller of the two.

'That's Bert.'

Her chipped fingernail moved to the older man standing next to him.

'And that's his dad.'

'Can I borrow this?' I asked, taking the frame from her unsteady hands.

'What for?'

'It will help with the article.'

'What article?'

She was now well and truly ratted, and it was obvious I wasn't going to get any more sense out of her.

'Can I take it?'

'Anytime you like.'

She pursed her lips and mouthed a kiss.

I slipped the frame into my coat and made for the door.

'Thanks, I'll see you get it back.'

I left her reaching for the gin again.

It took me ten minutes to reach the bus depot, where I had a stroke of luck. A bus had just pulled in and I asked the driver if he knew the whereabouts of Tickett.

'He should be in there having a cup of tea by now,' he shouted from his cab, pointing to a mess room at the back.

Dodging between a couple of parked buses I made my way to the back of the garage. A short, middle-aged man wearing a driver's disc in his lapel emerged bearing a distinct likeness to the chap in the photograph.

He confirmed his name, and I identified myself. 'I wondered if you could tell me more about the ammunition dump in Sessington – I was at the council meeting last night when they read out your letter.'

'Aye, it's reet enough, my old man put 'em there his'sen. He told me so.'

'That'll be on Jim Pargeter's land, then?'

He lit a cigarette and took a long drag at it before replying. 'That's reet, I suppose it is.'

'It would be a pity if the police were to dig up his garden just before Bridgefield Show, it would ruin his leeks.'

'Aye, poor old bugger – but best be on't safe side, know wor I mean, like?' He tried to smile, but his eyes refused to co-operate. I nodded.

'Are you showing at Bridgefield this year?'

'Always do.' His eyes could not remain still for a moment.

I decided to stop pussyfooting about. 'He says you are only doing this to wreck his chances.'

He looked hard at me and his tone took on an ugly note. 'Look mister, you'd best watch what you're saying. If you print that I'll have you before't magistrate.'

I put up my hands in mock surrender, I didn't want to antagonise him I needed his co-operation. 'OK, OK, I just want to get your side of the story. Did your father tell you what kind of ammunition was buried there?'

He took another drag and exhaled smoke through his nostrils.

'All sorts, mortars and the like, and they used to make a lotta home-made stuff.'

I took out my notebook and pressed him for more information about himself and his father, a farm labourer who during the war had been a corporal in the Home Guard. The old man had also been a keen gardener and taught Bert all he knew about growing prize leeks.

It was time for the soft soap treatment.

'It's an important story, Bert. You are doing the village a service by bringing it to the attention of the authorities. It would be nice to have a photograph of you to go with the story.' I could see the idea of being the village hero appealed. 'What time do you finish?'

'About half an hour ago. I'm on m'way home.'

'I'll get our photographer to call round later this afternoon. OK?'

He was silent for a couple of seconds, then nodded.

So far so good, now I needed to know what the police were doing.

Sally Falls' car was parked outside her police house when I got back to Sessington and she answered the door eating a sandwich.

'Lunch,' she explained, as she showed me into her small office. She sat down at her desk still munching away, and gestured to the chair opposite.

Over the past twelve months I had developed a lot of respect for WPC Falls. In her late twenties and always friendly and helpful, she had demonstrated a tough streak last year, when single-handedly she had arrested two violent thugs at Bridge-field Fair.

'Well what's the press after today?'

'An un-reclaimed ammo dump in the centre of Sessington,' I replied.

'Oh, that.' She sounded dismissive.

'Have you seen old Pargeter yet?' I asked.

'I called on him this morning, but there was no reply, and he wasn't in the garden. I'll have another go this afternoon.'

I recounted my meeting with him the previous evening and

asked what would happen if he refused to allow the police into his garden.

'We would have to get a warrant to search it. Technically he could be harbouring firearms without a registered permit.'

'He has to have a permit for something he doesn't know he's got?' I asked incredulously.

'That's the legal position.'

'And once you've got the warrant?'

'We dig up his garden.'

'Pargeter's been working that garden now for twenty-five years or so. If there was anything there he would have found it long ago.'

She nodded agreement. 'You are probably right, but we don't have an option. We have to respond to information received.'

'In other words by creating this red herring Tickett will sabotage Pargeter's chances at Bridgefield and keep his own hands clean.'

She shrugged. 'It's not our problem.'

A few minutes later I pulled up at Jim Pargeter's cottage where a group of onlookers had been attracted by Simon Robinson the local TV reporter and his film crew assembling their gear. He was talking to a local radio reporter.

I had spoken earlier to Harry Gorton. On occasions like this we link up as a freelance team, he supplying the pictures, me the words. He was looking thoughtful as he came to the car.

'Not much chance of a shot of the garden, Mark. There's a six foot wall round it.'

'Not to worry,' I told him. 'Just hang around and get snatch pictures when the police arrive.' I handed him the picture I had borrowed from Mrs Tickett and pointed out the old man. 'We'll need some copies made of him for the *Clarion* and the *Times*, and I've arranged for you to take pictures of Bert Tickett this afternoon. I need shots of him in his garden, next to his leeks.'

There was a flutter of excitement as Sally Falls' Fiesta pulled up, causing the TV cameraman and his sound lad to almost trip over each other in their haste to get ahead of her and start shooting her purposeful walk towards the cottage. Harry's motor driven Minolta also began working overtime.

She knocked on the front door. It opened immediately to reveal Jim Pargeter in his braces and collarless shirt, brandishing a garden fork. The policewoman's smile was designed to take the sting out of a bed of nettles, and she turned it on full beam as she greeted him.

'Hi, Jim. We've had a report that there could be some dangerous nasties in your garden. Can I come in and talk about it?'

'You can not.' His voice was loud and uncompromising. 'And if you try I'll have the law on you.'

Sally smiled again. 'Don't be daft Jim, I am the law. Come on, put the kettle on and we'll talk about it over a cuppa.'

'Tha's still not coming in.'

The WPC tried another tack.

'Jim, I know your garden means a lot to you, and I know how you feel about your leeks, but you could be in danger. Let's be sensible about it.'

The old man's eyes were burning with fury. 'There's no one coming rummaging in yon garden, and if they try they'll get this up their arse.'

He shook the garden fork in her face, and turning to the onlookers who had gathered, roared, 'And you lot can bugger off as well.'

With that he turned and slammed the door in her face. She tried knocking again but there was no response. Returning down the path she announced that the show was over and shoved the radio man's mike away as he asked her to comment.

It was starting to rain, so leaving Harry to drive over to Tickett's place I made a dash for the village tea shop. I was greeted by Bertha Sanderson the proprietor emerging through a beaded curtain, and asked for a tea.

As she poured from a large brown pot she eyed my notebook. 'You writing about our Jim Pargeter?' she asked disapprovingly.

I nodded. 'It's a good story.'

'It's a load of rubbish and you know it,' she scoffed. 'Bert Tickett ought to be ashamed of himself, and I'll tell him so when I see him.'

I couldn't disagree with her, but as a human interest story went, this had the lot and taking my tea over to a table in front of the window streaming with condensation, I began writing up my notes.

'A 76-year-old pensioner, thought by police to be sitting on an arsenal of unexploded bombs, barricading himself in his small cottage and refusing them access to search his garden. A former Durham miner thinking more about his prize leeks than his own safety, claiming he had been set up by his arch rival in an attempt to sabotage his chances at a local show. His rival alerting the parish council about the danger of the bombs placed there by the village Dad's Army. Widower Jim cultivating the land for the past thirty years and spending last nine months bringing his leeks to show standard. Nearby residents anxious about their safety and their property. Confrontation with woman police officer, and the police applying for a warrant to search the garden . . .'

It was all there, including quotes from Pargeter and Tickett, the police and the council as well as from some of the villagers. Satisfied I hadn't missed anything, I ordered another cup of tea, and crossed over to the pay phone and began dictating the story to the national newspapers. As I did so, Bertha Sanderson quietly busied herself behind the counter of the otherwise empty café, slicing and buttering scones, all the while listening intently as I unfolded the Jim Pargeter story to some distant copy-taker.

When finally I put the phone down and caught her disapproving look, I smiled as I returned my cup to the counter.

'I don't make the news, I only report it,' I declared.

'You only make trouble,' retorted the redoubtable Bertha as I disappeared through the door. I was just getting into my car when Harry pulled up alongside and he grinned across at me.

'Any problems?' I asked.

He shook his head. 'Tickett is lapping up the publicity. See you.'

He roared off to organise the transportation of his films.

'You look pleased with yourself,' said Jill, putting down an armful of shopping and flopping down on my knee. 'Like a cat in a dairy.' She rubbed my nose with hers.

'Do you fancy the Ellerthorpe Hotel tonight?'

'Pushing the boat out a bit, aren't we?'

'We can afford it. It's been a good day.'

Which was true. The local radio bulletins had led with the story from late afternoon, and it was the second item on the BBC's local TV early evening news programme. Simon had done a good job, the shots of Pargeter arguing with Sally Falls making particularly good footage. More importantly from a financial point of view, it was now a running story, which meant the papers would want a follow-up from me tomorrow when the police arrived with a warrant to search Pargeter's garden.

So that night we lived it up a bit with a few drinks, and an excellent meal at the plush Ellerthorpe Hall Hotel, and predictably I awakened the following morning with a thick head. It was Jill's day off and she was still asleep and leaning across the bed I gently removed a strand of her blonde hair which was lying across her lips, causing her to stir and turn over.

I staggered downstairs and made myself a strong coffee. A thump in the porch signalled the arrival of the morning papers and anxiously I spread them on the kitchen table and quickly flicked through them.

Neil Armstrong and Buzz Aldrin were still making the headlines with their first moon walk, but Pargeter had made an inside page lead in four of the tabloids and the story received prominent treatment in the rest of the nationals. Harry's pictures were terrific, especially one of Tickett in his garden with a smug smile on his face, holding aloft two giant leeks.

'Well,' said a bleary voice behind me, 'are you rich?'

Jill plonked herself next to me and pushing her hair to one side reached for the papers. I handed her a mug of coffee and together we began reading the coverage.

'Who's a clever boy, then?' she said finally, stretching across the table and kissing me firmly on the lips.

I grabbed at her, but she pushed me away.

'Oh no you don't, some of us have work to do.'

'You're off work today.'

'I'm not talking about me,' she teased.

She went upstairs to dress and I poured myself another coffee and considered the day's schedule. Once the police had their warrant I would need Harry to doorstep Pargeter's cottage, and, I had to know when they would serve it. I rang police headquarters and was put through to the press office where Peter Addison, with whom I had become quite friendly, answered.

'Morning Mark, you're on the ball aren't you? But there's no more information yet. You'll have to check with the General Hospital at Mallingborough.'

'The General? What the hell's a hospital got to do with a search warrant?'

There was a brief silence at the other end, then I listened to him in disbelief. 'Sorry, I thought you must have heard. There was an explosion in Sessington this morning, about half an hour ago. We have no further details, apart from an old man being rushed to hospital.'

Jill must have heard me shout 'Jesus Christ' because she came running downstairs urging me for an explanation. As I told her she grabbed the phone from me.

'You get dressed, I'll see what I can find out.'

I dashed upstairs and pulled on a sweater and trousers and by the time I had returned to the kitchen Jill was speaking to a nursing colleague in the casualty department.

She replaced the phone and said quietly, 'It's not good. He's almost certain to have lost a foot, and he's suffering from second degree burns and shock.'

'Do they know what happened?'

'No, only that there was an explosion.'

The area around Pargeter's cottage had been cordoned off by police tape when I arrived on the scene, and Sally Falls was having difficulty keeping villagers under control. Simon Robinson was already there with his TV crew, and the commercial boys were setting up an OB unit.

A young army captain appeared from the side gate of the cottage accompanied by a sergeant and a police officer. I ducked under the tape, followed them to a parked army Land Rover and showed my press card.

'What happened?' I asked.

'Take your pick.' The captain ticked the possibilities off on his fingers 'Mortars, grenades, and rounds of small arms ammunition. He probably disturbed one of the grenades, which in this case was nothing more sophisticated than an old milk bottle filled with white phospherous, which would have self-ignited when exposed to the atmosphere. They can cause fearsome burns.'

'Where were they buried?'

'Under the compost heap, probably the only area of garden he's never dug. He had probably figured this out for himself and decided to see if there was anything there.'

WPC Falls came over looking tired and strained.

'It looks as if we misjudged Bert Tickett,' I said.

'Well, it's academic now,' she replied. 'We've just been on to the hospital. Jim Pargeter died fifteen minutes ago.'

The shock must have frozen my expression. 'Are you all right?' Sally Falls gave me a close, worried look.

What did she expect? How does anyone look when they've helped to kill someone? I felt physically sick, shaken, ashamed. I'd exploited an old man for financial gain, and he'd paid with his life.

I saw Simon ducking under the tapes and coming towards me. 'Mark, can you arrange for . . .'

'Not now, Simon.'

I pushed past him and almost ran to the car. I drove home fighting a losing battle with my conscience. If the national spotlight hadn't been shone on Pargeter he might have been persuaded to have experts search his garden. But like many in Sessington I had convinced myself from the outset that Bert Tickett's motives were born out of resentment and jealousy, rather than out of any true concern for the old man. Tickett might have been persuaded to call on him and quietly discuss the potential danger. Pargeter might then have reacted differently. But I had encouraged the confrontational angle because it made a better story, better headlines.

Jill, the pragmatist took a different view.

'What would have happened if you hadn't broken the story?' she asked me.

'Jim Pargeter would still be alive,' I replied bitterly.

'Kids playing in that garden could have found that ammunition. What then? Bert Tickett tried to warn him, so did the police, and so did you. But Jim Pargeter chose to ignore the lot of you.'

I knew she was right, but the story I filed with the papers that afternoon lacked sparkle and was written with a heavy heart. I told Jill about Bertha Sanderson calling me a troublemaker.

'Yes, and I bet she's the first at the newsagent tomorrow morning to read the troublemaker's account of it,' she countered.

Two weeks later, motoring through Sessington, I passed Jim Pargeter's cottage again. A man was working in the front garden and as I slowed down I recognised Bert Tickett.

I stopped the car and went over to him.

He was reading my mind.

'Aye, he was proud of his garden was Jim, he wouldn't want

to see it go to rack 'n' ruin. I'll be keeping an eye on it till new owners take over.'

I wandered round the side of the house into the back garden. The police hadn't stinted their search, the entire plot had been roughly dug over, with the exception of one section which was now neatly raked, and planted, with leeks.

I heard Tickett behind me.

'He would have wanted it,' he remarked casually.

'Are they yours?' I asked, pointing to the leeks.

'Aye. Shame to waste good soil.'

He flicked his cigarette end in the direction of the once compost heap and, turning quickly, went back to the front garden.

I told myself that this man had done everything possible to warn Pargeter of the danger lurking here. Then I remembered Mrs Tickett's drunken outburst.

'He hates his guts,' she had said. 'He can't better Lucky Jim, can he.'

As I returned to the car I stopped, and looked back at Bert Tickett again.

He was smiling contentedly.

The Vicar and the Wife-swappers

It was in my local in Bardsey that I first picked up the talk of wife-swapping parties in Sessington, three miles down the road.

Harry Magnus, an incorrigible gossip, was holding forth on the subject as I ducked into the bar of the White Hart that night.

'Going at it like rabbits' he announced to his attentive audience. Jim Slater laughed and shook his head as he pulled me a pint. 'He makes it up as he goes on.'

'It's straight up,' said Harry indignantly as I took my beer and sat at one of the rickety tables.

'Starts with a drinks party on a Saturday night, then chaps throw their house keys in a bag and women pick 'em out and go off with their new partners for the night.'

'You been there and seen this for thi'sen Harry?' grinned Jim from behind the bar.

'Cleaning woman told my missus all about it.'

Bill Lundy, a farm worker whose marriage was a notoriously tempestuous affair, demanded, 'Where's all this swapping going on then, Harry?'

'Why, is tha' thinking of putting your Bessie in for another model?' retorted Harry.

No one took Harry too seriously, he had cried wolf too many times in the past, and I might not have given the matter a second thought had it not been for Edith Perth telephoning me the following day insisting I did something about the Revd John Blake.

'I think he's got a screw loose, I really do,' she said sounding slightly bewildered.

Blake's recent arrival at St Peter's in Sessington had caused quite a stir. At twenty-six he was the youngest vicar in the county and most of the parishioners, Mrs Perth in particular, had greeted his appointment with mild astonishment. 'He's nowt but a bit of a kid,' she had declared.

Despite his age, however, Blake was quite streetwise. From training college he worked as a curate in one of the most run down parishes of Burnthorpe, and with the vicar there had battled to inject a bit of self-respect into an area bedevilled by poor housing, endemic thieving, prostitution and drugs. They hadn't stood a chance, but Blake's enthusiasm and hard work had obviously impressed the Bishop.

'So what's he been up to?' I asked Mrs Perth.

'It's the water,' she said.

'What water?'

'The water he's using instead of wine.'

'I'm sorry Mrs P., you've lost me.'

'For the communion service. He says Jesus was a teetotaller and would never have drank alcohol, the gospels got it all wrong according to him. Then there's the scarf.'

'Scarf?'

'Football scarf. Manchester United.'

I was surprised Mrs Perth actually knew what the Man. United scarf looked like.

'He has it dangling from his neck instead of the usual black silk affair they normally wear. He says if Jesus was alive today he would be talking to masses, and would go about his ministry among football supporters. It's not right, Mr Devlin, 'im interfering with the Bible teachings and the like. It's not right at all.'

She was still muttering her annoyance as she put the phone down.

It sounded a good story, eccentric vicars always make good copy, and Mrs P's information was usually reliable. It was certainly worth checking out, so the following morning I went down to Sessington and found John Blake squatting outside the front door of the vicarage mending a bicycle puncture.

'Things a bit flat with you, are they vicar?' I joked.

He smiled and shook my hand. We had met briefly when I had written a couple of paragraphs on his appointment for the *Weekly Times*.

'I've been hearing about some of your interesting theological theories,' I began.

He grinned up at me. 'You mean you've been talking to Edith Perth.'

He dunked the inner tube into a bowl of water and watched for tell-tale bubbles coming from the leak, then marked the spot with an indelible pencil before drying the tube with a towel.

'Is it true you are using water instead of wine for communion?'

He smiled as he applied adhesive around the puncture and placed a patch on the tube. Then he straightened up.

'Fancy a beer? This can wait.'

I squeezed past a number of packing cases in the passage and followed him into the large kitchen. 'You'll have to excuse the mess. Actually I thought you were here for another reason.' He reached into the fridge and pulled out two bottles of light ale. Picking up two glasses and a bottle opener, he pointed me to an open door.

'Come into the study.'

I walked behind him into a small room dominated by a huge desk, covered in books, papers and files.

'Looks as if you're in need of a good secretary,' I suggested.

'It's a bit of a tip,' he admitted. 'I just haven't the time to tackle all the admin yet.'

We sat facing each other. I eyed him over the rim of my glass and I found it slightly disconcerting to be talking to a man of the cloth who was actually four years younger than me. He leaned back in his chair and his boyish face was serious.

'You're a newspaperman, you must have heard the stories circulating around the village.'

'What stories?'

'Come on, don't tell me you've not heard all the juicy rumours about the sex orgies going on in The Plains.' This is an exclusive housing development set back in woodland on the outskirts of Sessington.

I placed my glass on a file marked Church Expenses. Suddenly things were getting interesting. Perhaps Harry Magnus hadn't been shooting a line after all.

'I'm not interested in rumours, only facts,' I told him.

'Then you've come to the right place.'

'I had heard that wife-swapping sessions were going on. Is it true?'

'Yes. But not for much longer. I'm going to put a stop to it.'

I was intrigued.

'I happen to know who the culprits are. Some are actually members of this church. On Sunday I intend denouncing them all, by name, from the pulpit.'

'You wouldn't dare, surely. What about the laws of slander?'

'What about the laws of God?' he declared. 'This type of depravity has to stop once and for all, no matter what it takes.'

I was about to ask him how he had discovered what was going on when we were interrupted by a female voice.

'Cooey vicar, it's only me.'

'My daily woman,' he explained. 'She who battles unceasingly with my untidiness. In here Mrs Brown. The door opened and into the room stepped Dora Tickett.

'We have met,' she said curtly as Blake introduced me. Indeed we had, over a gin bottle on the tragic story of the old ammo dump under Jim Pargeter's compost heap. She was still wearing a tight sweater, but the short skirt I'd last seen her in had been replaced by a more sober ankle-length creation, and her hair was under control, tied back in a pony-tail with a cheap elastic band. She was also sober.

'You had better start in here, Dora,' said Blake, rising. 'Mr Devlin is about to leave.'

As he accompanied me to the front door I asked how long Bert Tickett's wife had been working at the vicarage.

'Wife?' He looked surprised. 'That's not Bert Tickett's wife, he's a widower. That's Dora Brown, his sister.'

It was my turn to show surprise. 'She lives on the council estate,' I said.

'No, no,' he corrected me. 'Dora lives alone in The Plains.'

Now I was totally confused. The large detached houses on The Plains are very expensive, and I was intrigued to know how the likes of Bert Tickett's sister could afford to live there. But it was obvious she knew what was going on and had confided in Blake.

I was so preoccupied with these thoughts that it was only when I got back to my car I realised that he still hadn't told me why he was using water instead of communion wine, and why he was wearing a football scarf rather than the conventional tippet.

I made a couple of telephone calls and bought vegetables for Jill at the general store before returning to the vicarage and parking outside. I didn't know how long Dora Whatever-they-called-her was likely to be, but I intended staying there until she came out.

When she finally emerged I watched her close the large iron gates before I wound down the window.

'Hello again,' I shouted. 'Can I give you a lift?'

She stopped and stared hard at me, then came over to the car and put her head to the window.

'Now I wonder why you would want to give me a lift?'

'Because it's beginning to rain, and it's a long walk to The Plains,' I replied, stretching over and opening the passenger door. But she ignored the offer and walked away. Then she suddenly stopped and came back to the car.

'All right, but can we call at Websters?'

'Sure, no problem.' I didn't have to guess what she would be buying at the off licence.

I drove to the centre of the village and pulled up outside the general shop once more, and waited until she returned clinking a carrier bag which she nursed on her knee.

'Do you mind if I have a fag? The new vicar doesn't like me smoking.'

She fumbled in the carrier and brought out a packet of the less expensive cigarettes and a cheap disposable lighter. She was obviously ill at ease and glanced at me furtively as if she wanted to tell me something but couldn't bring herself to say it. Finally she made up her mind.

'Look, the last time we met, I was . . .' She stared out of the windscreen.

Despite the lack of make-up, she had attractive features, but the drink was beginning to take its toll.

'You were drunk,' I smiled.

'I was stoned out of my mind,' she replied emphatically. 'I must have said some dreadful things.'

'Forget it, I didn't give it another thought.' I changed the subject. 'How long have you been working for the new vicar?'

'Since he arrived here.'

'He's going to blow Sessington apart on Sunday.'

She nodded. 'Serves the stuck-up buggers right.' It was said with feeling.

'You know about this wife-swapping business, then?'

Before she could reply I had turned into The Plains and she was directing me, not to one of the large impressive houses, but to the end of a cul-de-sac where she pointed to a small, very small, bungalow set back behind a privet hedge. It looked entirely out of place amongst the luxury properties surrounding it.

She was reading my mind. 'Looks ridiculous, doesn't it?'

'A little out of scale,' I agreed.

'They've never forgiven me for moving in here. They say it lowers the tone.'

'Who's they?'

'This snotty lot around here. They wanted the builder to pull it down when he finished the estate. But he owed me a big favour, and he stuck to his word.'

She could see she wasn't making much sense and as I pulled up in front of the small wooden gate, she turned and said, 'Look, do you fancy a drink or don't you?' She banged the car door shut and I followed her up the narrow garden path to the front door.

Once inside, she produced two glasses and pulled a bottle of gin from the carrier bag.

'Gently,' I warned as she poured.

The small living-room was tastefully furnished with a quality carpet and a small three-piece suite and occasional tables. A large picture window overlooked a huge uncultivated stretch of land.

'So what's all this about the builder?'

'My husband worked for him. He was a joiner on this estate.'

Her eyes filled with tears as she came across and stared out of the window into the middle distance.

'We had had a row the night before, over nothing, absolutely nothing, and we were still sulking and not speaking to each other when he left for work in the morning. When he didn't come home at teatime, I thought he was still in a huff and was probably in the pub with his mates. Then the police arrived. The top scaffolding hadn't been secured properly, and Brian had fallen fifty feet on top of a pile of bricks. He was, as they said, dead on arrival.' Her voice was now almost a whisper. 'I'll never forgive myself for that row. We did love each other. We didn't have much, but we were very much in love.'

Her face took on a haunted expression as she went over to the mantelpiece and took down a photograph of a nice looking chap whom I guessed was in his late twenties. She placed it on her bosom, and wrapped her arms around it clasping it tightly.

'There was all sorts of trouble with the builder's insurance.' Her voice was now weary as she replaced the picture. 'Brian and I were living in a rented cottage near the library and as part of the deal for me settling out of court, the builder – a decent chap really – agreed to turn the site office into this bungalow once the development was finished. I now own it, and the land out the back . . . Generous, sure. But it doesn't bring my husband back, does it?'

She lapsed into silence, until I asked quietly, 'So when did the neighbours start playing up?'

She lit another cigarette.

'I hadn't been here long when this bloke from down the road knocks on the door. Invites me to a party he and his wife are throwing. I thought they were just being neighbourly, I didn't know anyone around here, so I accepted. I didn't realise what kind of party they had in mind until it was too late. There were six couples, all from around here, and one chap by himself. I'd obviously been chosen to make up the numbers, a widow with big boobs and short skirt, they were onto a racing certainty, or at least that's what they thought. Anyhow, the booze flowed and everyone was as tight as a fiddler's elbow by ten o'clock. Then Tim brought in a sports bag and tossed his house key into it.'

'Tim?'

'Tim Lakes, the guy who invited me. The other five blokes did the same. Sandra Lakes, his bitch of a wife, then held up the bag and each woman dipped in for a key. You can guess the rest.'

'The men went back to their own houses, but with a different partner?'

'Yes, only I refused to take part, and that was when things started getting nasty.'

'In what way?'

'One woman called me a jumped-up slag, and another suggested I was on the game, then two of the men started groping me. I kneed one so hard I must have totally ruined his night. Finally I ran for the door, and came home.'

'When was all this?' I asked.

'About two months ago.'

'Why didn't you report them to the police? They could be charged for indecent assault or attempted rape.'

'No way,' she declared emphatically. 'That's what the vicar wanted me to do. But they would just close ranks. Anyway, two of the men are solicitors. Who would believe my story against theirs.'

'Are these parties still going on?'

'Oh yes, most weekends.'

'And have they troubled you since?'

'No. I went to stay with my brother Bert on the council estate for a while, but we didn't get on, and after that Jim Pargeter business I came back here.'

'So your real name is Brown?'

She nodded and began caressing her wedding ring.

'Which is Tim Lakes' house?' I asked.

'Number sixteen, the one with the matching Porsches in the drive.'

She suddenly became agitated. 'Listen, I'm not getting involved with any newspaper story, I just want peace and quiet.'

I got up and made towards the door. 'Take it easy on the gin,' I urged.

Number sixteen The Plains was straight out of *Homes and Gardens*, and Dora Tickett had been only half right: there was only one Porsche in the drive. I pressed the bell and heard chimes echo behind the glass door.

The young woman who answered was stunning, and she knew it. The combination of flashing blue eyes, flawless complexion and short dark hair was quite electrifying. Her figure had been poured into tight bottle-green corduroy trousers which were topped with an expensive cerise silk shirt with the top two buttons unfastened to create a cool casual effect.

'Mrs Lakes? Mrs Sandra Lakes?'

'Yes.'

The next part was going to be tricky, and I chose my words carefully.

'My name is Mark Devlin, I'm a reporter and I'm seeking public reaction to a story I have picked up from the local vicarage, and I wonder how you feel about it.'

'What story is that?' Her smile could have charmed birds from the trees.

'It appears that on Sunday the vicar is going to denounce certain villagers from the pulpit, he's actually going to name them, and I'm trying to find out what residents feel about such a personal attack?'

Her smile took on a slightly anxious line, but she managed to pose the question lightly. 'Why, whatever have they been up to?'

'It seems they have been indulging in wife-swapping parties.'

At that, blue eyes hit the panic button and her smile vanished, but only for a split second. By the time I had asked if she thought the church should get involved in such matters, she had recovered her composure.

'I'm sorry, I really can't help you. In any case we seldom go to church. Sorry.'

She closed the door quickly, and I saw the shadow of her back lean heavily against the opaque glass.

'How would you like to go to church in Sessington on Sunday?' I asked Jill that night. She looked up from her ironing, puzzled.

'What on earth for?'

I explained what had happened, and when I told her how Dora Brown had been treated, she couldn't wait to have Sandra Lakes and her friends exposed.

By Saturday, the gossips in Sessington were in their element and I spent a long time on the phone to the Courier and the news desks of the nationals discussing the story, which bristled with legal problems. The local television stations were grateful for the tip and Harry Gorton returned my call and we arranged the picture coverage.

When Jill and I arrived at the church that Sunday morning, it was already packed; the Sessington bush telegraph had obviously been working overtime. We squeezed into a pew about half way down the aisle and as I looked around I guessed there were many faces present that had never seen the inside of the building before.

I could see old Mrs Perth sitting in the second row, her maroon hat pinned firmly to her white hair, and close by was Dora Brown who turned and smiled. On the opposite side of the aisle about three pews away I also recognised Sandra Lakes sitting beside a tall, tanned, immaculately groomed man who I assumed was Tim Lakes, her husband. But it was the man next to him who interested me. John Thorston was a leading solicitor in Bridgefield, and I wondered if it was just coincidence that he was sitting there today of all days, or was he keeping a watching brief on behalf of the clients?

The choir preceded the Revd Blake who, to everyone's amusement, had his Manchester United scarf draped around his neck. It was so long the two ends almost touched the ground.

Jill nudged me as another figure came into view. 'You didn't tell me he was coming,' she whispered, and I too was surprised to see the bishop in all his regalia walking behind Blake. I picked up the order of service and discovered that three young men were going to be confirmed by the bishop.

As the processional hymn ended Blake turned to face the congregation. 'Before we start our morning service I have two announcements. Firstly . . .' He paused, and smiled. 'Last Sunday I must confess to having a major disaster. Just before our communion service I turned suddenly in the vestry, and my cape caught up in the wine rack containing four bottles of communion wine. The entire stock shattered on the floor. As it wasn't possible to replace them at such short notice, I'm afraid communicants last Sunday had to be content with receiving Sessington tap water. Thankfully the wine stocks have now been replenished. My second announcement concerns this.' He unwound from his neck the football scarf and held it aloft. 'I've been wearing this scarf most of the week in the hope someone would recognise it and claim it. It was found over a week ago in the churchyard. If anyone knows who owns it, perhaps they would contact me afterwards. Being a City supporter I find it embarrassing to say the least.'

His announcements caused a ripple of muted laughter and helped to relieve the tension. I looked over to Edith Perth, her face was inscrutable. After the bishop had concluded the confirmation of the three young lads, Blake slowly climbed the five stone steps to the pulpit and you could almost taste the suspense.

I took out my notebook.

Clasping the sides of the rostrum, he stared out at the upturned faces for what seemed an age, as if he was seeking to identify every member of the congregation individually. Then in a loud penetrating voice he started his sermon.

'My text this morning is taken from the fifth chapter of 1 Corinthians.' He paused dramatically, then reading from his notes, declared: ' "It is reported, that there is fornication among you." ' The dramatic silence that followed this pronouncement caused the woman beside me to gasp and place her hand quickly to her mouth.

'The Bible.' He held his book aloft. 'This good book tells us, and I quote, "If any person be a fornicator . . . with such person you should not eat." '

He glared at his audience, some stirred uneasily, others were wide-eyed and positively excited. This was precisely what they had come to hear. ' "Stolen waters are sweet, (pause) and bread eaten in secret is pleasant (pause) but lust not after her beauty, neither let her take thee with her eyelids. For by means of a whoreish woman, a man is brought to a piece of bread, and the adultress will hunt for the precious life." '

He was really getting into his stride now reeling off a tirade of biblical quotations to hammer home the same theme.

' "So he that goeth with his neighbour's wife, shall not be innocent. Can a man take fire in his bosom and his clothes not be burned? Those that commit adultery destroyeth their own souls." '

I glanced towards Sandra Lakes. She was as white as a sheet, and her eyes never left the neck of the man sitting in front of her.

Blake seemed to be staring down at her, singling her out, when he thundered: ' "For a whore is a deep ditch, and whosoever lieth carnally with a woman betrothed to a husband, shall be scourged." '

The bishop continued to stare into the middle distance.

But as Blake's vilification continued, there was still no mention of any actual names. He touched on all the problems licentious behaviour brought upon families, and how it eroded decent society, but he still had not mentioned The Plains. His reference to the citizens of Sodom and Gomorrah and how they had given themselves over to fornication and the desire of strange flesh and suffering the vengeance of eternal fire, was all good tub-thumping stuff, but it wasn't what the villagers had turned out to hear.

As the organist struck up the final hymn and Blake descended the pulpit steps there was a sense of anti-climax, and in some quarters not a little relief.

'What was all that about?' Jill whispered.

As we filed out, Blake and the bishop were standing either side of the porch shaking hands with the dispersing congregation.

'Was your shorthand up to it?' he asked me, grinning.

Jill, sensing that my frustration was about to make me say something regrettable in response, pulled me away.

I crossed the churchyard to where Harry Gorton and Simon Robinson and his camera crew were standing. Like me, Simon was spitting blood.

'You mean we've called a crew out on a Sunday for bugger all?'

'I'm sorry Simon, I trusted him, I really believed him.'

'Can't we salvage anything?'

He was thinking of his production budget and the double overtime of the crew.

'There's nothing to salvage, you heard him, just a load of hot air, not one name, not a single fact. The story is dead.'

As we drove home Jill placed a consoling hand on my knee. 'What I can't understand is why he mentioned it to you in the first place if he knew he wasn't going to go through with it. It's not very vicar-like.'

I remained silent, thinking furiously. When we arrived home I transcribed his entire sermon from my shorthand notes. It was after re-reading his quotations that the penny suddenly dropped.

I grabbed the telephone directory and began searching frantically through it.

'The cunning devil,' I shouted. 'He kept his word, he actually did it.'

Jill shot into my study. 'Did what?'

'He actually named them, look. I don't believe it, listen to this.'

I read one of his quotations from the transcript. ' "The whoremongers and liars shall have their part in the Lakes." Lakes, Sandra Lakes, get it? Here's another one. "For a whore is a deep ditch and a strange woman is a narrow pit." '

I pointed to the entry in the telephone directory: E. D. Pitt, 12 The Plains, Sessington.

'Look at this . . . "can one go on hot coals and his feet not be burned". J. K. Coals, 14 The Plains, Sessington.'

Together we roared with laughter as we worked through the sermon. He had them all. He had even named the area: 'He overthrew these cities and the Plains.'

Not a bit of wonder he asked me whether my shorthand had been up to it. 'Do you think Sandra Lakes would understand what he was getting at?' Jill asked.

'It doesn't matter, he's achieved what he wanted.'

'And what was that exactly?'

'In the first place, to put a stop to the shenanigans in The Plains which Dora Brown brought to his notice when she got the job as his cleaner. He knew I would follow up the story once I knew he was going to dramatically name the guilty parties, and when I called on Sandra Lakes I effectively did his job for him, didn't I? There is no way any of that lot are going to step out of line now they know the press have the story.'

'But more importantly he has prevented this scandal getting into the papers, because he knows I can't use the story now, I don't have any names or any quotes, and Blake is not going to admit to what he did this morning.'

Jill nodded. 'This guy is quite an operator.'

'You can say that again, because he also achieved what his predecessor failed to do as long as he was in Sessington.'

Jill suddenly realised what I was getting at. 'Yes . . . He's filled his church on the very day his bishop was visiting,' she said, her eyes burning in open admiration for the Revd John Blake.

'Exactly, and furthermore he ensured the media would be present, including the television cameras, which the bishop no doubt thought his blue-eyed boy had organised for his benefit.'

The phone interrupted us. It was Blake.

'Congratulations,' I said. 'I've got to award ten out of ten for style.'

'You cracked it, then.' He chuckled. 'I'm sorry about your story, but all is not lost.'

'How do you make that out?' I asked cautiously.

'Well, you missed the other story, the three young men who were confirmed.'

'What about them?'

'They were prisoners from the young offenders institution in Burnthorpe. I persuaded the authorities to let them out for the day. We also arranged to have six prison warders in the congregation, just to be on the safe side you understand. Have you got your notebook handy? Oh, incidentally I also took the liberty of telling your photographer who took some good pictures of the lads with the bishop and myself. Now, fire away, what would you like to know?'

Later that afternoon Simon Robinson rang me to make sure

I'd got the confirmation story. I told him how Blake had duped us, and he too saw the funny side of it.

'At least he saved the day for us and I understand two of the lads want to enter the church, leopards changing spots and all that.'

'Tell me Simon, did you ever come across Blake in Burnthorpe?'

'No, I gather that before he entered the ministry he was in advertising and public relations.'

I closed my eyes and shook my head. 'Now you tell me.'

'And incidentally, he asked me to tell you that Edith Perth, whoever she is, asks your forgiveness. Does that make any sense?'

I cast my mind back to Mrs P's telephone conversation with me, and I slowly nodded.

'Oh yes,' I replied. 'It makes an awful lot of sense.'

Sudden Departure

The thunderstorm that had been threatening all morning finally broke over Bardsey with such dark torrential ferocity I had to turn on the desk lamp in my study. With Jill at work I had the house to myself and was busy writing a report on a previous evening's council meeting when my thoughts were interrupted by the doorbell.

As I opened the door I couldn't help but smile.

Boy, was she wet. She was so drenched she looked as if she had just been pulled out of the river. Her thin red anorak had offered no protection against the storm, neither had the sodden jeans which were flattened against her legs, and the rain had plastered her long blonde hair against her forehead, giving it a saturated shine. With water dripping from her glistening face, she leaned her bicycle against the porch.

'I need an outboard motor if I'm going to get home,' she announced, pulling a large brown envelope from her saddle-bag and handing it to me.

'This is for you. I'm Emma Proudfoot.'

She stood inside the porch and shook her head like a dog coming out of a stream.

'I think I'm coming up for the third time,' she quipped.

'Here, give me that,' I insisted, peeling her out of the dripping anorak revealing her equally soaked T-shirt which clung in such a sensual manner to her attractive young figure it was obvious she was wearing nothing beneath. She kicked off her soggy

trainers and followed me inside, leaving a trail of damp foot-
prints on the carpet.

'I thought I could beat the storm and anyway Dad wanted
you to have it today. It's his book on Sessington, he hopes
you'll review it in the *Clarion* and the *Times*.'

I nodded. Cllr. Ann Scrolls had telephoned me about this
book. Evidently she had helped Alan Proudfoot to proof read
it. 'It's quite brilliant Mark, I think you'll be impressed,' she
had said.

I knew Proudfoot was an estate agent in Bridgefield, but
apart from that I knew very little about this tall, good-looking
guy. Edith Perth had once told me he was 'one of your born-
again Christians' which hadn't impressed her one bit: 'Didn't
know what the inside of a church looked like six months ago,
and before you can blink they've made him church warden.'

I took the book from his daughter and placed it on the table.
'You didn't have to make a special journey, I'm in the village
most days, I could easily have collected it.'

She shivered as a searing flash of lightning illuminated the
room, followed by the roar of thunder overhead.

'You've got to get out of those wet things or you'll catch
your death. Come on.'

Meekly she followed me upstairs through the bedroom where
I pointed her towards our en suite bathroom. Whilst she stood
there looking like a drowned rat, I took a bath towel from the
airing cupboard and laid it on the stool next to the shower.
Returning to the bedroom I dug out one of Jill's sweaters and
a pair of jeans.

'While you are returning to dry land I'll ring your father
and tell him you are here.' I handed her the clothes.

'Actually he's my stepfather,' she corrected. 'Do these belong
to your girlfriend? Kate says you aren't married, you just live
together.'

'Who's Kate?' I asked.

'My mother. She's an artist. Very good, too.'

I closed the bathroom door.

Downstairs I dialled Alan Proudfoot's number. There was no reply. Returning to the study I threw a couple of logs on the fire and tried to concentrate on my report.

'Do you know where your girlfriend keeps her hair-dryer?'

I turned, and was quite taken aback at the sight of this ravishing young teenager standing in the doorway loosely wearing my short dressing-gown which had slipped off one shoulder. She had draped her hair round the other shoulder and was towelling it dry. Then seeing the fire slumped on the rug before it.

'Never mind . . . this'll do even better.' She dropped her head towards the flames.

'I take it the gear was a bit on the large size.'

'Enormous. This is much more comfortable.'

She hugged the dressing-gown and bent her head forward again. This time the movement allowed the dressing-gown to gape at the top allowing me an unhindered view of her firm attractive breasts. Turning suddenly, she caught me looking, and smiled.

'I've telephoned your house and there is no reply,' I told her.

'Alan's at work and Kate will be painting. You've got to let it ring.'

I went back into the hall and dialled the number again.

'Kate Proudfoot,' said a soft voice finally.

'Mrs Proudfoot, I'm Mark Devlin, your daughter has just delivered me a book.'

'Did she get there before the rain?'

'No, she was soaked to the skin, and at this moment she is sitting in my study drying out.'

Emma came up behind me and took the phone from my hand. 'Hi Mum, be an angel and bring the car round, and something for me to wear.'

She smiled into the receiver as she listened to her mother asking questions, and chuckled up at me as she replied, 'His dressing-gown, would you believe.'

'She'll be here in ten minutes,' she announced, replacing the phone.

'Would you like some coffee?' I asked.

She followed me into the kitchen. We sat at the kitchen table drinking coffee, her blue eyes never leaving mine for an instant, which I found disconcerting at first. But as she quizzed me about my work, I became almost seduced by her flattery. She was a most self-assured young lady, whose manner was that of a mature woman, yet she couldn't have been much more than sixteen.

We both heard the car turn into the lane and watched Kate Proudfoot's shooting-brake pull up at the front gate. She was much younger than I expected, late thirties I guessed, average height, slim, dark short hair, nice features. And there was no disguising the concern in her eyes as I opened the door and she saw her daughter standing next to me, drinking coffee and wearing nothing but my loose dressing-gown. I had this uneasy feeling she thought she had interrupted something rather beautiful.

'My, you must have been wet.' Her greeting to Emma held a touch of irony.

'Soaked to the skin.'

'So I can see.'

Emma pointedly pulled the dressing-gown tighter as her mother stepped into the passage.

'Here, you'd better get into these.' She handed her a sports bag.

'Can I use the bedroom again, Mark?' Emma asked.

I experienced another pang of unease, and searched Emma's eyes for a clue as to why she had posed the question in such a provocative manner.

'Yes, sure.' I replied hastily, then turning to Kate, 'I've just made coffee . . .?'

She pre-empted the invitation. 'No, no thank you. I want to make the best of the light.'

'Yes – Emma told me you are a painter, and a very good one at that.'

I suspected she wondered just what else Emma had been telling me.

She was cool to the point of being offhand, and I was pleased when the atmosphere was broken by Emma, looking fabulous in a tight sweater and jeans, skipping down the stairs stuffing her wet clothes into the bag. Turning to me, she flashed a high-octane smile. 'Thanks for drying me out, Mark.'

'Thank your father for the book.'

I helped load her bike into the back of the shooting-brake, while Kate Proudfoot, ignoring both of us, got in behind the wheel.

Within half an hour the storm had passed and I took the car to Sessington to post an article I had written for one of the farming magazines. Jill's car was standing outside when I returned.

'Hi, I'm back.'

Seeing her face I knew she was less than pleased.

'Something wrong?' I asked her.

'You could say that.'

Her tone had all the chill of an Icelandic trawler. From behind her back she produced a pair of women's skimpy knickers.

'Well?' she demanded.

'Well what?' I asked confused.

'Perhaps you can tell me what these were doing on our bathroom floor.'

The penny dropped. I explained about Emma Proudfoot's visit.

'And just how old is this girl who leaves her visiting card in our bedroom?'

'About sixteen, seventeen.' I was becoming uneasy under her interrogation. 'Listen you don't think . . .' I gave a dismissive laugh. 'You think I've been having it away with this girl, don't you?'

'I'm still waiting to hear what these were doing in our bedroom.'

'Bathroom,' I corrected.

Although she finally accepted my explanation, I could see she was still sceptical.

'You must be raving mad,' she stormed. 'You invite a nubile young woman into the house and encourage her to take her clothes off. Good God, man, did it never cross your mind what dangers you were creating for yourself? You of all people, the worldly journalist who's seen it all. One wrong word from her, and it will be you who will be splashed all over the Sunday sleaze.'

'Come off it,' I responded equally angry. 'The kid was soaked to the skin.'

'A seventeen-year-old is not a kid,' she ranted. 'A seventeen-year-old, is a woman.'

I knew she had a point. I recalled Emma's provocative smile when she had caught me looking down at her in front of the fire, and I couldn't make up my mind if leaving her pants behind had been accidental, a schoolgirl prank, or a blatant act of encouragement.

'So what are you suggesting?' I demanded.

Before she could answer we were interrupted by the doorbell, and flouncing down the passage she threw open the door to reveal a tall gaunt figure in a filthy black torn overcoat. His long greasy hair merged with his greying beard and he looked as old as Methuselah. He was soaking wet.

'Couldn't spare a few coppers for an old man down on his luck, could you, ma'am?'

He crossed his arms around his waist as if to protect himself from the cold, his rheumy eyes were bloodshot and above his beard his skin was like parchment. Yet surprisingly his voice was cultured, with the bronchial undertones of a heavy smoker. He must have been amazed by Jill's response.

'Of course, of course, come in, come in.' Her exasperated tone was loud and shrill as she held the door wide open.

'Jill . . .' I warned.

But it was too late, the tramp had stepped inside, looking quite bewildered.

'It's our day for taking people in, isn't it, Mark?'

Her smile was pure saccharin.

'Don't just stand there Mark, I'm sure this gentleman would appreciate some coffee and a change of clothes, wouldn't you?' And turning on her heels she flounced upstairs leaving me to deal with him.

The old man shuffled uneasily, aware that he had stumbled on a domestic row.

'That's very decent of you, ma'am' he mumbled after her.

'You had better come in here,' I said, leading him into the kitchen.

He sat uncomfortably on the edge of his seat nursing a large newspaper parcel which clanked when he put it at his feet.

'You from these parts?' I asked, handing him a mug of coffee.

He shook his head 'No, just passing through.'

He drank the coffee gratefully and helped himself to the biscuits I had put out.

Jill returned to the kitchen carrying a couple of my sweaters.

'Are these any use to you?' she asked him.

His eyes lit up when he saw them, and he glanced anxiously at me. I shrugged. 'Very kind of you both,' he wheezed.

He reached for his soggy parcel which split open as he picked it up, revealing a battered old alto saxophone. Intrigued, I put out my hand and took it from him. It had certainly seen better days and I could just make out that it was a Buescher made in the States in 1914.

I handed it back to him. 'Nice instrument,' I acknowledged, wondering where he had got it. 'Can you play it?'

He looked hard at me for a moment, as if he had taken offence at the question, then slowly placed the mouthpiece between his lips and moistened the reed.

It's often said the saxophone takes on the voice and the personality of the player, and as the rich breathy notes of a simple tune reverberated around the kitchen, they perfectly mirrored this frail, sensitive figure who was producing them so beautifully.

When he finished, no one spoke, until finally Jill said softly, 'Thelonious Monk, "Around Midnight". We have the record.' He nodded, and began an improvisation on the same tune, but this time developing a new theme, cascading notes like water spilling from a mountain stream which I finally recognised as John Coltraine's 'Giant Steps'.

'Thank you sir, bless you both, and the best of luck to you,' he said as he left.

The episode helped to clear the air between Jill and me and that night in the White Hart I asked around about the tramp, but no one had seen or heard about him.

The following morning I had just finished dictating copy to the *Clarion* when the phone rang and I felt a pang of anxiety as I heard a voice chuckle.

'I think you might have something of mine,' Emma's voice was dark and husky.

'Jill found it on the bathroom floor,' I said, not knowing whether to adopt a stern, or a light, throw-away voice.

'My goodness. Was she very angry? Well, a girl does need her knickers,' she laughed. 'I'll ride out and collect them later this morning.'

'No,' I replied, rather too quickly. 'I'm just about to leave.' I lied. 'Jill will drop them off for you.'

I was pushing my luck because Jill had left me in no doubt about her feelings when she had used her thumb and forefinger to remove the offending garment and at arm's length had dropped it into the waste bin under the sink.

'I've put you out enough already.'

'It's no trouble,' I replied.

'It was very good of you to look after me yesterday,' she said, then adding softly, 'It was quite romantic really wasn't it? The thunderstorm, and the log fire and all that?'

Jill had been right. I had taken a big risk with this frisky teenager who now, somehow, would have to have her underwear returned.

Thoughtfully, I replaced the receiver, and went into the kitchen and opened the waste bin. Holding her briefs induced a sexual intimacy which worried me, and returning to my desk I stuffed her pants into a large brown envelope and contemplated my next move. The whole business was fast becoming a total farce. But in view of Jill's warnings and Emma's attitude over the phone, I knew I would have to tread carefully. I considered returning them to her stepmother Kate, but remembering the look on her face when she arrived to find Emma in my dressing-gown I quickly discounted that idea.

Half an hour later the decision was taken out of my hands when the doorbell rang and I found Emma on the doorstep looking ravishing in a tight black sweatshirt and thigh-hugging jeans. Her hair was pulled back in a pony tail and she was wearing just a hint of make-up.

'I was passing anyway, so I thought I would save you a journey,' she smiled innocently.

'Look, Emma, you've caught me at a bad time, I've got to dash. Hang on a second.'

I almost ran back into the house and snatched the envelope from my desk. But as I turned she was standing next to me.

'Yours, I believe,' I smiled, handing her the parcel.

Without taking her eyes of me she ripped it open and took out the briefs and held them in front of her crotch.

'Do you think they suit me?' Her eyes dared me to look.

I tried to keep my voice light and unconcerned.

'I'm sure they suit you admirably, now I've got to go.' I guided her by the shoulder to the front door where she suddenly turned and kissed me passionately on the lips, her tongue tingling mine.

Before I had a chance to recover, she had mounted her bike and ridden up the path. At the gate she turned and blew me a kiss and disappeared down the lane.

Still savouring the taste of her lipstick, I cast an anxious glance up and down the lane desperately hoping no one had seen us, then still shaken, I returned indoors, only to find the brown envelope and the briefs lying in the passage.

I dashed to the gate with them, but I was too late, she was already out of sight and I ran to the car and caught up with her on a quiet stretch of the road to Sessington.

'You forgot these,' I shouted through the window. She pulled up and, laying her bike on the grass verge, came round to my side of the car. I handed her the envelope and made sure she placed it in her saddle-bag.

She laughed. And putting her head into the car she kissed me quickly on the lips and pulled away smiling, then seeing an approaching tractor she pressed herself to the car to allow it to pass, at the same time pushing her pert breasts into my face.

'But you could have dropped them off any time, you are always in the village aren't you?' She arched her eyebrows provocatively and I slipped the car into gear and waved goodbye through the window. In the mirror I saw her standing in the middle of the lane laughing and returning my wave.

Over the next couple of days I tried to persuade myself that it was only because Jill was on nights and our paths hardly crossed that I didn't tell her about Emma's second visit. In any case, I told myself, there had been nothing to it, she had just been passing and had taken the opportunity to collect her property; anyway, it was pointless opening old wounds with Jill. But that night I returned home to find Jill in the kitchen talking to PC Ted Jenkins from the Bridgefield nick.

'Emma Proudfoot has gone missing,' she told me quietly.

I felt my heart go into overdrive. 'When?' I asked, pulling up a chair and sitting opposite them.

'She went to a friend's house in Sessington around teatime yesterday. When she hadn't come home by ten thirty, Mrs Proudfoot rang the house and discovered she had never arrived.' PC Jenkins looked up from his notebook. 'According to Mrs Proudfoot, Emma visited you the day before yesterday.'

'Yes, she sheltered from the thunderstorm and Kate Proud-foot came and collected her about four o'clock.'

'Did she appear upset, or concerned about anything?'

I shook my head.

'And have you seen her since?'

It was the question I had been dreading, and I flashed a glance at Jill who was watching the officer writing everything down.

'As a matter of fact I did, she came back the following morning, to collect . . . an envelope she had left.'

Jill's look could have welded me to the wall.

'An envelope?' I had dealt with Jenkins on a couple of stories in the past, and found him a hard-nosed ambitious copper, whose tone of voice always suggested he didn't believe a word you were telling him. 'Did you know what was in the envelope?'

I saw Jill, tight-mouthed, staring at the ceiling. Yet there was no way I couldn't reveal the contents because Kate Proudfoot had probably already told him anyway.

'An item of clothing.'

His eyebrows arched. 'What kind of clothing, sir?'

I took a deep breath. 'Her panties.'

The next twenty minutes were among the most uncomfortable of my life as Jenkins subjected me to a barrage of searching personal questions aimed at establishing a relationship between Emma and me, and the look on Jill's face was enough to tell me she believed this to be the case. With her eyes burning into me I tried to answer his questions calmly. But the tenor of his questions made this difficult.

'What I don't quite understand sir, is why her . . . pants . . . were on the bathroom floor in the first place.'

'Because she had been taking a shower. She was soaking wet.'

'A shower, you say?' He made it sound like a scene from a blue movie. 'And she finally took her . . . er . . . clothing home with her when she returned alone the following day.'

I nodded, and he finally closed his notebook. But I had the distinct feeling he was far from convinced.

After he had left, Jill didn't give me an opportunity to explain, preferring instead to storm upstairs and lock herself in the bedroom. I tried reasoning with her, but she was having nothing of it and I returned downstairs, furious.

OK, I knew I had been stupid in not telling her about Emma's second visit and I was angry with myself for putting our otherwise trusting relationship under strain, but I expected Jill to give me the benefit of the doubt. As for Emma, I was very angry that she should have placed me in this ridiculous position, while at the same time I was anxious about her whereabouts.

'She's probably shacked up with a boyfriend' said Nick Towel who was manning the *Clarion* news desk that night, and it was an opinion shared by Peter Addison the press officer at Bridge-field police station when I contacted him for an update early the following morning.

'It wouldn't be the first time a kid of her age has decided to run away from home. But it has been forty-eight hours without a sign of her. Let's say we are keeping an open mind.'

Which is more than could be said for the tabloid news editors, who sensing a juicy abduction story, despite my low-key report, were already dispatching their crime reporters to Sessington and instructing me to assist them in every way.

I had spent a restless night in the spare bedroom, and Jill, obviously still unforgiving, had left for work. I sat down with the morning papers and to my horror the *National Echo* had splashed Emma's disappearance, dressing up the story in the paper's inimitable style, building tension into it in a manner I would have done had I not been personally involved with Emma. I'd simply reported a young girl, last seen cycling around the village, had gone missing, and police were making the usual enquiries.

But what sent a wave of panic through me was the fourth paragraph quoting Fred Arundle a farm worker who had seen

Emma talking to a motorist in a lonely lane near Sessington. If this were true it was odds on he had recognised me as the driver. Arundle worked on John Briggs' farm and knew practically everyone in the village.

I heard a car pulling up outside and my heart sank as I watched WPC Sally Falls walking up the path, accompanied by a man wearing a leather jerkin.

'Hello Mark. This is Detective Constable Bell. We need to have a talk.'

It was pointless denying the newspaper report. I had nothing to fear if I stuck to the truth, I kept telling myself. But it was pretty apparent that I was being interrogated as a suspect.

'What we can't understand,' said Bell, not taking his eyes off me for a second, 'is why you didn't tell PC Jenkins about this development.'

Farce was now fast turning into a nightmare.

I went through the entire story again and when I had finished Bell said simply, 'We would like you to come to the station and make a formal statement.'

'Are you arresting me?'

'Of course not, but we do need to have a full written account in your own words. You can follow us in your own car if you like.' Sally made it sound like a dinner invitation.

I scribbled an angry note to Jill telling her I was about to be arrested, and left it on the carpet in the hall. Twenty minutes later I was sitting across a table in an interview room in Bridge-field police station relating yet again my involvement with Emma Proudfoot, this time to Sally Falls.

When she had finished writing it all down she read it aloud to me.

'Is that a true record?' Seeing me nod in agreement she turned the statement towards me and indicated where I should sign it. As I handed it back to her, the door opened and DC Bell beckoned her outside. She returned moments later, looking shocked and strained.

'Can I go now?' I asked.

She looked hard at me, her pale blue eyes searching for my reaction. 'Emma Proudfoot's body was found in a ditch in Bramble Lane twenty minutes ago.'

'Dead?' My voice was no more than a whisper.

The beautiful vibrant teenager with the mischievous eyes and the long fair hair who had kissed me with such passion, dead in a ditch. It made no sense. It just wouldn't sink in. 'How?'

'We don't know yet.'

But her expression suggested I was now involved in a murder case.

I shook my head in disbelief and minutes later still in a state of shock I walked past the front desk.

'Mark, you old bugger, how you doing?' I recognised the voice and the burly figure of Bill Simpson the *Daily Post's* chief crime reporter who detached himself from half a dozen national reporters. 'Is this story going the distance?'

The rest of the pack came over and as I told them that Emma had been found dead, I suddenly became the centre of attraction.

'Where is this lane?' they asked almost in unison.

They followed me to the end of the village where we found the police had already sealed off Bramble Lane and there was no way Insp. Bert Yarrum was going to let us through. The only snippet of information he was prepared to impart was that an elderly man walking his inquisitive dog early that morning had discovered Emma lying face down in a ditch.

We stood around as the panoply of a major police investigation unfolded before us. The flashing camera of the police photographer was at work beneath a temporary tent and I felt sick at the thought of Emma lying there. Dr John Walden, the police surgeon, was talking earnestly to the pathologist, whilst the forensic team in their white disposable overalls shuttled between the tent and a blue Transit van. The news had travelled fast, and knots of villagers began assembling at the end of the lane and Inspector Yarrum barked to a police constable to move people on. He beckoned me and came across to the tape.

'You can tell your mates that we'll hold a press conference at the station at three o'clock.'

'Do you know what the cause of death is yet?'

'Three o'clock,' he repeated firmly.

I went back to my car and sat there trying to muster the energy and inclination to develop this story for the *Clarion* and *Weekly Times*. I knew it was only a matter of time before the pack followed up the *National Echo*'s story and interviewed Fred Arundle. To protect my back, I had told them that I too had seen her cycling that day, but it all depended on whether or not Arundle had recognised me, and whether the police announced that I had been helping them with their enquiries. Either possibility would sink me without trace.

I looked back at the mob of photographers and reporters and felt sick at it all. They had probably never given a second thought to Emma lying there under the police tent. She was now subordinate to the main media contest for the best words and pictures which would reap rich rewards. It was the story that was now all-important; now it was all about what people had seen, heard, or how they were feeling. Death, in media terms, is all about the living.

I knew most of the newshounds would be searching for Alan and Kate Proudfoot, and I knew that I too would also have to intrude into their grief for background material on Emma. I reached their house and found a posse of reporters and television crews hanging about the front gate. The show was well and truly on the road.

I drove home. It was almost one thirty, and I hoped Jill was back from the hospital. I needed her. What I didn't need was the tramp who had called on us three days earlier – sitting now in the kitchen with one foot in a bowl of water and Jill on the floor attending to what seemed a very swollen foot.

'He's turned his ankle,' she explained. 'I found your note. What was it all about?'

'We need to talk,' I said, and taking her hand I led her into the lounge.

She must have known by my voice and the look on my face that there was something seriously wrong. 'What is it, Mark?'
'Emma Proudfoot is dead. She was found this morning.'
'Oh God.'
She crushed her cheeks with her hands and flopped onto the settee. I went to the sideboard and poured us a couple of stiff brandies.
'What did you mean in your note, about being arrested?'
I recounted the events of the morning. When I had finished she got up and put her arms around me and held me tightly.
'They don't really believe you had anything to do with it?'
It was more a statement than a question, and I tried to allay her fears by telling her I'd only been helping the police with their enquiries, but my anxiety was palpable.
'What about the Proudfoots? They must be devastated.'
'Not at home. No one has seen them.'
We heard a cough from the kitchen.
'What's he doing here?'
'I found him sitting at the side of the road, he can hardly walk. There is nothing broken but he's got a very bad sprain.'
'What are you going to do with him?'
She shot me a guilty look. 'I told him he could stay here until the swelling went down.'
'What! And how long is that likely to be?'
'A day, a couple of days. Don't worry, I'll look after him, he won't be any trouble.'
I poured myself another brandy, and followed her into the kitchen where the tramp was sitting quietly, his face like parchment, his eyes half closed.
Jill, still in her nurse's uniform, dropped down on her knees and lifted his thin white leg and examined his swollen foot.
'I'll need to strap this, and you'll have to lay it up for a day. But if you are going to stay here you'll need to have a bath, and there will be no smoking. Give me a hand, Mark.'
Together we hoisted him onto his one good foot, and as he teetered there, we took off his stinking overcoat and grimy

jacket. He was a pitiful sight standing there in his tattered vest, trousers tied round his waist with an old leather strap. We put his arms around our shoulders and helped him to hop up the stairs to the bathroom.

'Look,' I said to Jill, anxiously glancing at my watch. 'I do have work to do.'

'OK, you can leave him to me now, I'll call you if I need any more help.'

Downstairs I began writing, and as I finished dictating my copy to the *Clarion*, I heard Jill coming downstairs.

'Where is he?' I asked.

'In the spare bedroom, resting.'

I followed her into the kitchen and she started preparing soup and sandwiches. As she worked over the stove, I put my arms around her waist and nuzzled her neck. She turned and kissed me, and I could see the anxiety in her eyes. 'You don't think there was anything going on between Emma and me do you?'

She shook her head. 'No, but why didn't you tell me that she had been here again?'

I gave a helpless shrug and she flung her arms around me.

I parked my car in Bridgefield high street and walked the few yards to the police station. A policewoman directed me to the canteen where the press conference was to be held. The small room was already crowded when I arrived and I had to squeeze past the television crews at the back of the room to find a seat next to Harry Gorton.

On the stroke of three o'clock the door opened and Insp. Yarrum, accompanied by WPC Sally Falls entered the room. They took their places behind a trestle table which suddenly was bathed in artificial light as the television crews switched on their equipment.

Yarrum consulted his file. He gave the basics – time, place and so on – then added, 'A post-mortem was carried out around midday and this revealed that Emma sustained injuries consistent with a hit and run accident. We are appealing for anyone who was in Bramble Lane who might have seen anything on the evening in question to come forward.'

'Bloody hell,' breathed one national reporter. 'All this for a sodding road accident.'

The Inspector explained how Emma had been struck a glancing blow which had hurtled her into the deep ditch and in the process she had broken her neck. He put the time of death around seven o'clock. I asked the usual question, about what she was wearing, whether the police had any leads, and the national boys chipped in with a few desultory queries. It was obvious they had been anticipating a juicy abduction story; a road accident would only receive a few lines down page.

For my part, I was so relieved that it wasn't a murder case, I couldn't wait to get to the pub on the other side of the street and file a rewrite of my earlier story to the *Clarion*. Bill Simpson was already at the bar.

'Make it two pints,' he said to the barmaid as I joined him. 'Can't win them all, Mark, but thanks for your help anyway.'

As I expected, Emma received hardly a mention in the nationals, and the *Clarion* only used four paragraphs from my report. I began to feel a little more relaxed – until Jill answered the door to DC Bell.

'Is this your car?' He pointed to my MG standing in front of the house. 'Mind if we take a look?'

'Help yourself.' I walked to the gate with him and noticed a police van parked there.

'Are these forensic?' I asked him.

'We just want to eliminate vehicles from our enquiries.'

They spent half an hour going over my car, and when they had finished, Bell came over and said, 'Thanks for your cooperation.'

'I didn't knock her down,' I told him.

I went back into the house and was pleased to see our vagrant visitor hobbling around with the aid of a stick. He looked a different person dressed in a pair of my slacks and sweater, he'd shaved and his hair was clean and under control.

'How's the foot?'

'Much better, thank you sir. I'll be away by tomorrow.'

He followed me into my study. 'You're a reporter then.'

'That's right, a freelance.'

'You'll have been a bit busy then, what with this accident like.'

'You could say that. You'd better take the weight off that leg.'

He sat down and eased his injured foot onto a stool.

'How did you come to sprain it?'

'Had to jump out of the way of a bloody idiot in a car.'

'Where was this?'

'On the back lane out of Sessington.'

'Bramble Lane?'

'Aye. They were taking the bend too fast.'

'They?'

'A bloke driving, a woman next to him.'

I was alert, the antennas working overtime. 'Did you get a look at them?'

He shook his head.

'It was getting dark, and I was too busy jumping out of the way. I thought he'd broken my leg, pain was so bad I could hardly walk, so I spent the night in the hedge back. A blessing your missus came along the following morning, a right angel she is.'

'This is important. A young girl was knocked down and killed in that lane. Think back, what kind of car was it?'

'Wasn't a car, it were one of those tall four-wheel drive jobs.'

'Like a Land Rover?'

'Aye, that was it, a Land Rover. Do you think it knocked down that young girl?'

I reached for the phone. 'Who's to say, but the police will certainly want to know about it.'

Inspector Yarrum was grateful for the tip and asked me not

to let our tramp go until one of his officers came over and took a statement.

'Can't you wait until they come?' Jill asked anxiously when I told her of the new development.

'Sorry darling, I've got to go. The *Clarion* and the *Weekly Times* are crying out for a picture of Emma, and the only way I'll get one is by persuading the Proudfoots to loan me one.'

The Revd John Blake was emerging from the Proudfoots' front door as I pulled up. Behind him I could see Kate Proudfoot standing in the doorway, and as I walked up the path Blake barred my way.

'I really don't think Mrs Proudfoot is in any state to receive visitors from the press,' he said firmly.

'Perhaps she should be the judge of that,' I replied equally forcibly, stepping around him. I felt his hand grasp my shoulder and I turned on him angrily. From the doorway Kate Proudfoot shouted.

'It's all right John, leave it, it's all right.'

For a second Blake and I stared at each other belligerently, then reluctantly he released his hold, but he followed me to the front door, and over my shoulder said, 'Kate, I don't think this is wise.'

'I've got to cope with it sooner or later, John. I'll be all right.'

'You are quite sure?'

She nodded.

'All right, but I'll be back in half an hour.'

She opened the door wider and stood silently to one side as I stepped into the hall. Without a word, she led me into a light, sparsely furnished room which had obviously been turned into her studio. A half completed picture of Sessington high street stood on an easel and on a table were miscellaneous sketches, a pallette and tubes of paint. Crossing to the fireplace she took a packet of cigarettes from the mantelshelf, toyed with it, then put it back. Her face, void of make-up, was grey and drawn and she had aged about ten years since I'd last seen her with Emma the day of the thunderstorm.

She combed her fingers through her short hair. 'How did you find out?' Her voice was edged with despair as she stood motionless, looking out of the window on an unloved garden carpeted with fallen leaves.

I wasn't sure what she meant.

'About what?'

'About Alan.'

Now I was confused. 'What about him?'

She put a hand to her forehead, hiding her eyes. 'Oh God.' She began sobbing uncontrollably, staring blindly at me as she wept.

'I can't handle this. Hold me, please God, hold me,' she pleaded.

I moved to her quickly, and pulled her towards me, and felt her tears. For what seemed an age I stood there, tightly holding her slender heaving body, and stroking the back of her hair, waiting for her sobbing to subside.

Finally she pulled away, her swollen eyes still pleading for help. I led her to a chair and handed her a tissue from a box on the table. She mopped her eyes and blew her nose. She tried to smile, but the tears were still flowing. My hand was around her shoulders and she covered it with hers.

'Thanks,' she said simply. 'I just needed . . . someone.'

I remained silent, holding her damp hands in mine, as she struggled to regain some sort of control. When she finally spoke, I just wasn't prepared for the bombshell.

'You didn't know did you? About Alan. He's dead.'

She said it so simply, in such a matter-of-fact tone, that for a second or two I thought I had misheard her, and that she must be referring to Emma. But then she began repeating his name over and over again.

'Alan,' she sobbed. 'Alan . . . Alan . . .'

I couldn't believe what I was hearing.

She struggled to her feet and crossed to the mantelshelf and this time she took a cigarette from the packet and lit it with shaking hands, then struggled with the words as she told me how John Blake had found her husband, the church warden, in a fume filled vehicle in the vicarage drive that morning.

'He thought the world of Emma, we both did.' She pressed her head into my shoulder again and her weeping turned into a long low wail.

From the front door I heard a voice call, 'It's only me, Kate.'

And as John Blake entered the room and saw the state she was in, he stood to one side of the open door.

'I think you have outstayed your welcome, Mr Devlin,' he said pointedly.

'Why the hell would he top himself?' demanded Jack Hopper, the night news editor at the *Post*, after I had filed my story later that evening. In common with most of the tabloid editors he was wondering if it had been premature withdrawing his staff men off the Emma story.

'He'd lost a daughter, perhaps he couldn't live with his grief.'

'Come of it, she was his stepdaughter.' The cynicism of a hard boiled newspaper man was bubbling to the surface and I instinctively knew what he was thinking. 'He wasn't having it off with her, was he?'

In my mind's eye, I saw Emma, mischievously parading her briefs in front of me, asking for my approval, and the passion with which she had kissed me. It would have been so easy to have returned her advances.

'Jack, if she was, we'll never know now.'

'Pity, it would have made a great story.'

The following morning our visitor left, still hobbling slightly as he went down the lane wearing my clothes and carrying in his parcel the provisions Jill had given him. When the papers came, Alan Proudfoot's suicide had produced the predictable crop of tabloid headlines, all on the 'churchman found dead after stepdaughter tragedy' theme.

The double tragedy plunged Sessington into collective shock

and mourning. I wanted to see Kate again, not in the role of a journalist picking over the bones of the story, but as someone who was genuinely concerned about her. The curtains of the house were drawn, however, and there was no response to my knocking at the door.

As I walked back towards my car I noticed Edith Perth ahead of me.

'Can I give you a lift?' I asked pulling alongside her.

'You're wasting your time if you're looking for Kate Proudfoot,' she announced as she got in beside me.

'Do you know where she's gone?'

'I do, but I'm not having you pester the life out of her.'

I told her the last thing I wanted was to harass Kate Proudfoot. 'The story's dead . . . I'm sorry, that was a poor choice of words. I just wanted to know if I could help in any way.'

She turned on me angrily. 'You could have kept the story out of the papers, for one thing.'

'You know I can't do that, Mrs P.'

'Poor lass.' She turned to look out of the windscreen into the middle distance as I drove up the high street.

'Poor man,' I answered.

'Bloody hypocrite,' she exploded.

I was shocked. It was the first time I'd ever heard Mrs P. swear. It was out of character. 'Why do you say that?'

'Save your sympathy for those that deserve it, I'll not be weeping for Alan Proudfoot.'

The words spilled out with such vehemence that it was very apparent she knew something that I didn't. My previous night's conversation with Jack Hopper came to mind, and I decided to take a flyer.

'Well, everyone knew he was having an affair,' I said offhandedly.

'All except his wife,' she declared.

'Always the last to know,' I agreed. 'Did you know her?'

She rounded on me and held my gaze. 'Yes, but you obviously don't.'

'And you aren't going to tell me, are you?'

'Right again,' and she lapsed into grim silence for the rest of the journey.

When I returned home that afternoon Jill had left me a message to contact Dora Tickett, and when I rang her it was obvious she and Edith Perth had been talking.

'Kate Proudfoot asked me to contact you. She doesn't want to see you or anyone for that matter, but she has asked me to say thank you for the other day.'

'Is she staying with you?'

She remained silent.

'How is she?'

'How do you think?' The bitterness in her voice was unmistakable.

'Dora, was Proudfoot having an affair?'

The line went dead.

The following day I had booked my car in for a service at Sean Kelly's garage, and as I pulled up the cheery Irishman came out of his office and greeted me in his inimitable manner.

'Marnin' Mark. A fine piece of scrap metal you've brought me here, so it is.' He kicked the tyres of my ten-year-old MG. 'A man of words like yourself should be driving one of them.'

He indicated a Land Rover parked at the back of the garage.

'I didn't think you were into car sales, Sean.'

'To be sure I am not. I'm garaging it for the police. But it'll be up for sale in due course, and going for a snip, you'll see.'

'I bet,' I laughed. 'Not if it's one of theirs.'

He cocked his head to one side. 'Wasn't the police who owned it. 'Twas poor fellow who gassed himself.'

'This was Alan Proudfoot's car?'

He nodded solemnly.

Suddenly our tramp's words about the Land Rover almost knocking him down came back to me.

'What were the police doing with it, Sean?'

'I don't know that Mark, but the men in white overalls were all over it.'

I walked down the high street to the telephone box outside of the post office and put in a call to the police station at Bridgefield and spoke to Insp. Yarrum.

'We are still pursuing our enquiries,' he told me after I asked if he'd had any success in tracing the vehicle that had knocked down Emma. But from his unenthusiastic tone, I had a distinct feeling that as far as he was concerned the case was closed.

'You mean it was Alan Proudfoot who knocked down and killed Emma?' Jill was wide-eyed at my news.

'It's a theory, only a theory.'

'But it does make sense doesn't it?'

I agreed. There was no doubt the police forensic lads could prove Proudfoot's Land Rover had been responsible for Emma's death, but with the owner no longer around I could understand their reluctance to give high priority to the case.

'If you are right, then who was the woman with him that night?' Jill asked.

'Good question. And were they having an affair? And if so did Kate Proudfoot know?' I remembered Edith Perth's bitter outburst when I'd mentioned Alan Proudfoot to her.

'Perhaps he genuinely didn't realise he had knocked Emma down,' said Jill. 'God how awful. Can you imagine killing your own stepdaughter. No wonder he couldn't live with himself. You aren't going to make anything of it, are you?'

'No. For one thing it's all supposition, and to be honest I just don't have the heart for it.'

And so Alan Proudfoot took his secret with him to his grave. At least I think he did. About six months later I was chatting to Edith Perth at a village function in the church hall.

'I had a letter from Kate Proudfoot the other day,' she announced.

I knew Kate had sold up and left the area shortly after Alan and Emma's funerals, but I had no idea where she had gone to.

'She's living in Bath, and teaching art at a girls' school. She seems to be coping with her new life.'

I told her I was pleased to hear it, and if she was writing back, to send my regards.

'You never told me who the other woman was, Mrs P.'

'No and never will. There's been enough trouble in this village to last a lifetime.'

At that moment we were interrupted by old Reg Parkes, clerk to the parish council, who touched me on the shoulder.

'You'll have a council by-election to report shortly, Mark.'

'Oh? Who's retiring?'

'Retired,' he corrected. 'Ann Scrolls. She's already gone, and her house is on the market. It was all very sudden.'

'Bitch,' retorted Edith Perth savagely, and looked me straight in the eye as she said it.

Hive of Political Intrigue

The immaculately groomed young woman behind the reception desk flashed me a smile.

'Can I help you, sir?'

'All right, June,' a voice behind me interrupted. 'I'll deal with Mr Devlin.'

I turned and saw Mary Walker sweeping toward me. 'Mark darling, it's lovely to see you.'

She pecked me on the cheek, embracing me in a cloud of expensive perfume, and linking my arm led me towards the hotel lounge where a tough-looking guy in a lightweight suit was standing.

'It's OK,' she assured him. 'This is Mark Devlin, a friend of ours. Show your press credentials, darling.'

'Again? I've just been through all this at the main gate.'

I dug into my inside pocket and gave him my press card. He checked the photograph with the real thing and courteously handed it back.

'How are you coping with all this hassle?' I asked her.

'God, I'm stressed out.'

She flopped into an armchair and raised a hand towards a young man in white shirt and black bow tie hovering in the background. 'Stephen, bring us some coffee, please.' She turned back to me. 'I'm really on edge about tonight.'

'I must say you don't look it,' I laughed. She was looking gorgeous in a navy suit, immaculate white silk blouse with a matching polka dot scarf. Her tan and the highlights in her long chestnut hair suggested a recent holiday in the sun. 'How's Jack coping?'

'Poor darling, doesn't know whether he's coming or going. He'll join us shortly.'

She followed my eyes as I watched a group of security men with Alsation dogs wandering through the lounge. 'Don't even ask. I don't. They arrived yesterday, the place is crawling with them.'

'Well let's face it, it's not every day of the week you have the Chancellor of the Exchequer to stay.'

She grinned at me, her eyes shining. 'It is one hell of a coup isn't it?'

As she poured the coffee she shook her head as if in disbelief. 'It's a far cry from those early days, Mark. There was a time, you know, when we thought we had made a huge mistake.'

'Can I use that quote in the piece I'm doing for the *Clarion*?'

'Is this the advertising feature we are paying for?'

I nodded.

'I don't see why not. We had more than a few sleepless nights in those days I can tell you.'

I reminded her about the shaking of heads in Sessington when she and Jack had announced they were selling their comfortable detached house in the village and putting the proceeds and their savings into an enormous mortgage to buy Ellerthorpe Hall.

'Yes. Everyone thought we were mad at the time, but we were convinced the Hall would make a super country house hotel. The top end of the market was crying out for it.'

'How difficult was it maintaining that vision?' I asked, reaching for my notebook.

Thoughtfully she nibbled at a rich tea biscuit.

'When things got really rough, and the bookings we'd forecast didn't materialise, we were tempted to drop prices and go down-market. The bank wanted us to do just that, they wanted turnover at any price. We had some pretty harrowing meetings with them I can tell you. Jack insisted we kept our nerve, but it was a very dodgy six months. The turning point was when we persuaded Peter Franks to join us.'

'We watched his programme the other night,' I told her. 'Jill has even tried out a few of his recipes.'

'He comes over very well doesn't he? Amazing what television exposure does for a chef. He has a tremendous following, we even get people now coming up from London for his cooking.'

I felt a strong hand on my shoulder and turning, looked up at a grinning Jack Walker.

'Anyone fancy a drink?'

'Its only half past ten in the morning for heaven's sake,' Mary laughed.

'I don't care if it's still breakfast time, I need a Scotch. No?' Mary shook her head. 'I'll stick to coffee, but I'm sure Mark will join you.'

'Just a beer Jack. Thanks.'

'How many are you expecting tonight?' I asked Mary as Jack went up to the bar.

'The place will be heaving. It's amazing how many bums the Chancellor puts on seats at a banker's dinner. Our limit is three hundred, but we could have doubled that. The press tables are at the front of the room, incidentally.'

'That makes a change, but I don't think many of the financial correspondents will turn up. His speech was released this morning and it doesn't contain anything contentious. What time does he arrive?'

'Around mid afternoon.'

When we had finished our drinks Jack showed me around the new extensions that were just finished. I had to hand it to the Walkers, they certainly had made a superb job of Ellerthorpe Hall and as Jack showed me the new stylishly furnished bedrooms he could see I was impressed.

'It's not bad, is it?' he admitted.

It was then, as we stepped out into the corridor, that we heard the strangled scream.

'What on earth . . .' muttered Jack.

He walked quickly to the head of the staircase, me alongside. We found Mary standing in wide-eyed terror with her back to a bedroom door, grasping the handle as if her very life depended on it.

'Whatever's the matter?' Jack demanded.

Her head gave a nervous tic towards the door.

He thrust her to one side and grabbed the handle. Together we rushed into the room and split seconds later we tumbled out again, having performed the quickest U-turn on record. The room was alive and dense with thousands of bees with clouds more coming in through the open window.

It was Jack's turn to hang on to the door handle. 'My God, this is the Chancellor's suite.'

The three of us stood there looking at each other. Mary, white faced, produced a pass key from her handbag and locked the door. Jack said, 'We need an expert, someone who knows something about bees. Mark, you must know someone.'

Off the top of my head the only person I could think of was old Fred Jarvis in Bardsey. He lived alone in a tiny one-up, one-down cottage in the centre of the village and officially he was employed by the local council as grave digger and custodian of the churchyard. Unofficially he was the person villagers turned to when an unsocial crisis arose, like a blocked cesspool, or a jackdaw trapped down a chimney, or when a drive needed repairing or when moles were playing havoc with somebody's lawn. He was also an accomplished poacher, selling the odd pheasant and salmon to anyone not too fussy about where they'd come from. In short, old Fred was a typical rural character, part of the village fabric, but did he know how to deal with a swarm of bees?

'I think he's your best bet,' I said. 'I'll ring Jim Skelton at the White Hart. I know Fred does odd jobs there, and Jim pays him in beer.'

Mary was now recovering her composure. 'Jack, close the windows everywhere. And don't let anyone up here or mention this to anyone. My God, what a disaster, today of all days. You can use the phone in the office, Mark.'

Jim Skelton chuckled when I got through to the White Hart and explained the Walkers' predicament. 'Aye, Fred's here in't garden.

'Jim, keep him there, we'll come and get him.'

'I'll go,' said Mary. 'I'll need to clear him with the security people.' In seconds her BMW was trailing dust down the driveway.

Jack and I went to the first floor and checked the bedroom windows. Satisfied they were all closed, we returned downstairs, and opening the door to the kitchen Jack almost collided with Peter Franks on his way out carrying a milk bottle with about twenty bees inside.

'I've been catching these damn things all morning, I don't know where they are coming from. No sooner do I catch one, than another half dozen appear.'

Jack took him by the arm and led him back into the kitchen.

'What!' he exclaimed when Jack told him of the bees in room four. 'That's the Chancellor's suite.'

Jack looked anxiously around the kitchen where the staff were busy preparing for the big dinner. 'Quiet, Peter. We must not let this get out.'

'Let it get out?' spluttered Peter. 'You're standing next to a reporter, for God's sake.'

'Mark's all right, he's a friend.'

'Hang about, Jack,' I retorted. 'I do have a living to earn. Anyway, you're panicking unnecessarily. It's a lovely human interest story and providing it's handled properly it could give you some great publicity.'

'Oh, sure,' he said ruefully. 'I can see the headlines now – Chancellor Evacuates Killer Bee Hotel.'

The sound of the BMW interrupted further comment, and the three of us dashed into the lobby as Mary, looking hot and dishevelled, opened the door and quickly ushered in the shuffling figure of Fred Jarvis.

He was wearing pinstripe trousers at least two sizes too big for his small frame, hanging at the crotch like a horse's nosebag and secured at the waist by a dressing-gown cord. His top half was clad in a Fair Isle sweater which had shrunk so badly it gripped his chest like a tourniquet. On his feet were muddy Wellington boots turned down at the tops, in one hand he carried a large cardboard box with a lid, and in the other a battered grey top hat around which had been secured a piece of bride's wedding veil.

He hadn't a tooth in his head and when he greeted us with a flashing of his gums, his breath almost pinned the three of us against the wall. It occurred to me he was either going to immobilise the bees by simply breathing on them, or he was going to take the easier option and just stand there and frighten them to death.

Taking us to one side Mary said, 'Fred says he can catch them.' Her voice had a strangled quality; driving him here in a warm car had obviously taken its toll.

'Good,' said Jack. He pointed to the staircase. 'After you, Fred.'

'Er . . . Mrs Walker . . .' The security man needed assurance.

'A problem with a blocked toilet,' she whispered in reassurance.

Laboriously Fred preceeded us up the stairs, each step causing his trousers to sag dangerously even further, and by the time he had reached the landing the top of his lilywhite backside was clearly on show. Pausing only to place the top hat on his bald pate and adjust the white veil, he gave a final hoist of his pants, and we watched disbelievingly as this bride of Frankenstein disappeared into the bedroom.

He re-emerged a few seconds later shaking his head.

'Can't do 'owt until they squat.' By this, we were given to understand the bees had not yet settled. 'Best come back in a hour,' he reckoned.

'An hour!' exclaimed Mary. 'The Minister is due at four.'

I checked my watch, it was two thirty. 'Can't you put him in another room?' I asked.

'No chance.' said Mary despairingly. 'We're fully booked and he's got to have the suite.'

Suddenly we missed Fred.

'Where's he gone?' cried Mary.

We turned to see him shuffling his way downstairs, his trousers almost winning the race to the bottom.

Mary ran down, took the old man by the arm and led him towards the office behind the reception area. At the sight of the advancing Fred, the receptionist leapt to her feet in horror.

'June, get Mr Jarvis a glass of beer, will you.'

The request was overridden by a commotion outside as two limousines pulled up.

'Oh my God, he's arrived early,' gasped Mary propelling Fred into the office. 'Jack do something.'

Jack did the only thing possible. Going to the entrance he stuck out his hand and extended a warm welcome to Ellerthorpe Hall to the Rt. Hon. Timothy Richards, Her Majesty's Chancellor of the Exchequer. He then proceeded to introduce this distinguished guest to Mary, Peter Franks, and June the receptionist. Then turning to me, Jack said; 'And this is Mark Devlin, a very close friend of ours.'

I shook the rather damp hand of the Prime Minister's right-hand man.

'I am also a journalist, Chancellor.'

He continued to smile. 'Which paper do you represent?'

'I'm the accredited man in this area for most of the nationals, and I cover for the local *Clarion* and *Weekly Times*. I would be most grateful if you could spare me a couple of minutes of your time.'

Before I could press further, his Personal Private Secretary, a sour looking man in a smart dark suit, interrupted dismissively. 'The Chancellor will hold his press conference at 4:30 as arranged.'

'I appreciate that,' I replied. 'But it would help my deadlines if I could have a word before then.'

As I was speaking, I could see over his shoulder Fred emerge from the office and amble his way towards the stairs. I knew Mary had seen him too, and I thought her composure was about crack.

Next to the PPS stood the Chancellor's press officer, a friendly looking guy about my age and to whom he now turned. 'What do we have lined up, Harry?'

The press officer consulted his notes. 'The man from the *FT*, two local radio interviews, a couple of regional television spots . . .' he ran his finger down the list, 'and Mr Devlin here will be handling the rest.'

'In which case,' smiled the Chancellor, 'we must spare a little time for Mr Devlin.' He moved towards the lounge, followed by his retinue.

'Can I get you a little refreshment, Chancellor?' Jack enquired.

'A little brandy and soda would be very nice,' replied the VIP, slumping into one of the armchairs.

I took Jack to one side. 'Make the most of it upstairs,' I whispered. 'I can't keep him here very long.'

I was now in a real predicament. International finance is the domain of the economist and the specialist writer, and I had always given the subject a wide berth. I hadn't a clue what to ask the Chancellor. Reporting his speech later that night would be no problem, I would just follow the press release, but now face to face with this illustrious politician, I needed to ask some sensible questions. Jack brought over a large brandy and placed it with a soda fountain next to the Chancellor, and with the eyes of the PPS and the press officer watching my every move I felt for my notebook and searched desperately for an opening question.

'Tell me, Chancellor,' I smiled, trying to emulate those confident inquisitors on television, then lamely asked, 'Is this your first visit to this area?'

'It's a few years since I was here, but I still own fishing rights on the river. We used to shoot around these parts. Used to stay with a farmer friend called Briggs.'

'Not John Briggs at Overacre Farm?'

'Good Lord yes. Do you know him?'

'Very well. He's chairman of Bridgefield District Council.'

'Is he indeed. Always was keen on politics, as I recall.'

'It will make his day when I tell him the Chancellor of the Exchequer was asking about him,' I laughed.

The sour PPS coughed discreetly and I stared at my notebook for inspiration. Finally I asked the question that interested me most as a house owner with a mortgage.

'Chancellor, you recently raised interest rates by a full one per cent. How do you think that will affect those people struggling with their mortgage repayments, especially in areas like this where there is high unemployment?'

It was a question Jill had asked me when the new rate was announced and it prompted an immediate response now. He turned on his fiscal tap and I sat back and allowed the words to wash over me.

'. . . I'm not claiming that the level of real long-term interest rates is the most important economic indicator, but they do reflect an important judgement by financial markets about future economic stability which take into account various factors such as the level of short-term interest rates, future fiscal policy, wage agreements, and inflation forecasts . . .'

I only hoped Fred was winning his war with the bees.

'While real interest rates, which as you know are interest rates adjusted for inflatory expectations, are rising throughout the world'. . . . there was no stopping him now . . . 'There remains the question as to why they should have risen to different degrees in Europe . . .'

The PPS was nodding sagely while this diatribe was going over my head. I glanced helplessly at the press officer; he smiled, and I detected a flicker of a wink.

'There is a press release I can let you have on this interesting subject,' he offered.

I thanked him. 'That would be most useful,' I said gratefully. I tried keeping my end up with a series of basic questions on the economy, and when Timothy Richards finally rose, I reckoned I'd managed to give Jack and Mary a twenty-minute breathing space.

A smiling Mary came over. 'If you are ready, Chancellor, I will show you to your suite.'

'That's most kind of you, Mrs Walker.'

Then I saw her freeze as we watched Fred wheezing his way across to us, still carrying his top hat with the veil around it.

'Jack,' Mary called helplessly.

But before Jack could cut him off, he came over and stood directly in front of the Chancellor. 'Gawd damn me, I thought it was . . . Mr Timothy.'

Richards stepped back and raised his eyebrows, then a slow smile broke over his features. 'Fred Jarvis,' he roared, and he shook the old chap's hand so hard I thought Fred's breeches might fall down again.

The PPS looked as if his master had stepped into something rather nasty, and Mary and Jack just stood aghast.

'Fred, my dear chap – are you still with the shoot?'

Fred shook his head and gave his toothless grin. 'Nay, it's me bronchials, Mr Timothy, couldn't keep up these days.'

Turning to the assembled company Richards beamed. 'This man . . .' He put his hand on Fred's shoulder. 'This man was the best gamekeeper we ever had. Saved my life once, remember, Fred?'

Fred continued to stand there grinning. 'It were nowt,' he chortled.

'Nowt he says. Let me tell you, if it hadn't been for his presence of mind when I fell onto some barbed wire and cut an artery I might have bled to death. It was the tourniquet that Fred put on, that saved me. I'd never have lasted to the hospital without that.'

I couldn't believe what I was hearing. 'What a wonderful story, Chancellor. Have you any objections to me writing a piece on you and Fred meeting up again like this?'

'Of course not. Time I had some good publicity. Clear it with Brian first.'

His press officer looked pleased, but the PPS looked as if he was having a particularly bad nightmare.

Mary finally stepped in and rescued Richards from Fred and led him and the PPS to the VIP suite.

'What about the bees, Jack?' I asked.

'Gone,' Fred interrupted.

'You're kidding.'

Jack looked equally perplexed. 'It's right. There wasn't one left.'

'Scout bees must have found a better site,' Fred announced happily. 'They was just resting up.'

'They chose the best bloody bedroom in the house to do so,' Jack replied bitterly.

'But why would they want to swarm in a bedroom?' I was completely baffled.

''Tis the colour, likely as not,' rasped Fred.

Jack was equally mystified. 'What's wrong with the colour. We've just redecorated that room.'

'All blue.' Said Fred. 'Bees go for owt blue.'

'Get away,' said Jack.

''Tis a wonderment,' Fred opined.

He contorted his toothless features into a grimace that would have won him first prize in any gurning competition, and wandered happily towards the door.

'I'd better get him back to the White Hart,' said Jack.

'Not before I've talked to him about his derring-dos with Her Majesty's Chancellor.'

Later as I cleared the story with Brian Fellows, the press officer, over a drink at the bar I told him about the problem with the bees, and that I intended using it in a lighthearted fashion.

'Sounds as if it's been your lucky day.' he grinned. 'Anyway, the Walkers shouldn't have worried. The Chancellor is an authority on bees. Keeps a dozen hives on his farm in Kent.'

A week later Jill and I received a parcel by special delivery. Inside was a huge salmon.

'For being a B . . . good sport,' read the accompanying card from the Walkers.

When I rang Jack to thank him, he chuckled.

'Don't thank me, thank old Fred. I bought it from him when I finally dropped him off the other day.'

'I don't suppose he told you where he got it?'

'No, and I didn't dare ask,' he laughed.

The Law Truly is an Ass

Jill passed me the *Weekly Times* over the breakfast table, and pointed her half-bitten piece of toast at the report on the recent Bridgefield council meeting.

'Have you seen this?'

I lowered my copy of the *Clarion* and adopted a tone of patient despair.

'Not only have I read it, my darling, but if you recall, I actually wrote it.'

'You didn't tell me this prat was getting up people's noses again.'

It wasn't the first time Sir James Drummond, chairman of the Bridgefield County Council, had captured the local headlines. This tall, handsome, autocratic man in his late forties, had a reputation for rubbing people up the wrong way.

He had taken over the Bridgefield Manor estate on the death of his father Sir Harold Drummond who had been the Member of Parliament for this region for over twenty-five years. Drummond junior was a commanding figure who considered the chairmanship of the council the family right, and he treated his fellow councillors and officials as members of his personal staff who were expected to support every decision he made. He was also a very successful businessman, and as well as farming the estate had numerous other business interests and served on the boards of at least three major companies.

Not a man to welcome interference or criticism, he refused

to get involved with the media, unless of course, he thought he could benefit from so doing.

In fairness, some of his ideas had benefited the town, but his latest crusade to enhance the appearance of Bridgefield high street was going to upset a lot of people.

Drummond had concluded that many of the shop displays were getting out of hand and some of the decoration and fascia signs were becoming too flashy and flamboyant. Much to the dismay of the shopkeepers he had decided they were now contravening local planning laws. Incredibly, he had instructed the Chief Planning Officer to enact his powers and prosecute the offenders unless they came into line.

'He's nothing more than a damned dictator,' said Jill. 'Surely he can't get away with this?'

She took the paper back from me and re-read the report.

'Is he right . . . about violating planning regulations and breaking the law?'

'Technically yes, if they have altered, or put up signs without planning permission. Bridgefield happens to be in a conservation area.'

'I still say Drummond's a prat.' She continued reading the report, getting angrier by the minute. 'You've got to do something about this, he's even objecting to Harrisons having bunting and balloons over their door, he wants the neon signs on the butchers taken out, and – listen to this – Ted Bolton's new chemist sign is considered to be out of all proportion to the surrounding environment. I don't believe this, listen, Slatcher's Café have been told to remove their fairy lights and Henry Childs the ironmongers will have to take in their display of ladders and garden furniture from the pavement because it represents a safety hazard. The man's a fool, the high street has been like that for as long as I can remember. It's part of the attraction.'

I grinned at her. 'You are so sexy when you're mad.'

I had every intention of following up the story that very

morning. It had all the ingredients of a first-class row, and I knew many of the traders were already spitting blood over Drummond's interference, but later that morning as I was about to set off for Bridgefield the phone rang and I recognised the voice of Nigel Carnaby.

'Can we meet?'

Now, when Carnaby rings, I'm always on my guard, because it usually means he wants some publicity, invariably for himself, so I didn't commit myself straight away.

'What is it, Nigel? I'm a bit pushed for time.'

'It's about our friend Drummond, I've just been talking to a few traders in the high street.'

'Oh yes.'

I knew his wife Angela had a dress shop in the high street, and perhaps Drummond's planning directive would be affecting her.

'Yes, I think we should talk,' he went on.

'OK, I'm listening.'

'No, not over the phone. Let's meet in the Three Jugs at 12:30?'

As I replaced the receiver, it instantly rang again.

A woman's voice asked, 'Mark Devlin? Sally Broomfield, Kevin Johnson's secretary at the *Clarion*. Mr Johnson would like a word.'

To say I was surprised was a serious understatement. I had never met the influential Managing Director of the *Clarion* and the *Times* newspapers. He had taken up his appointment after I had left to go freelance.

His voice was loud and authoritative, and he had decided we were on first name terms.

'Is that you Mark? I wonder if you could spare me a few minutes later this afternoon.'

Intrigued, I asked what it was about, but he cut me short.

'I don't want to discuss it over the phone, shall we say 4:30?'

'What was that all about?' Jill asked after I had replaced the receiver.

I shrugged. 'Search me.' I replied.

According to rumour Nigel Carnaby was a millionaire umpteen times over, but unlike Drummond who enjoyed inherited wealth he had amassed his fortune from his own labours, building up a very successful scrap business in nearby Ellerthorpe before selling out to an American conglomerate. He and his wife now lived in a large detached house on the outskirts of Bridgefield. He wasn't everyone's cup of tea. In truth he was cocky, arrogant, and fearlessly opinionated, but never one to duck a challenge, and always prepared to strut his tubby figure into any controversy going.

He had only been in Bridgfield five minutes when he put himself up for the local council, against Sir John Drummond no less. Drummond had been dismissive of the arrogant newcomer, which almost backfired on him, because Carnaby did surprisingly well in the polls, and much to Drummond's anguish, forced a recount, before the 'Big Drum' as he is known locally, squeezed home by only thirty-eight votes.

I had been singled out for Carnaby's special attention once he learned I was the local press man, and Jill and I were always the first to be invited to the parties he and his wife regularly threw for the great and the good in Bridgefield. He had been particularly attentive to me when much to the chagrin of the local council he and Angela decided to form the Bridgefield Civic Society to keep a voluntary eye on the town, looking after its trees and planting bulbs on the Green, and generally keeping the place tidy.

Carnaby's heart was in the right place however, and as I turned into the side street and pulled up in front of the Three Jugs, I knew that if he was getting involved in the high street row, there would be a story in it.

Tucked away between two white stone cottages, the Three Jugs is the smallest, the oldest and certainly the most uncomfortable, pub I've ever been in. Bobby Watson, the cheerful little man who owns it, once told me the original building had been a cow byre, and some would say it had lost nothing in the conversion. Yet despite its claustrophobic low ceiling and spartan outside lavatory, the Jugs is adjudged to serve the best ale in the town.

As I ducked into the empty room, Bobby called his customary greeting from behind the old oak bar, on which stood a barrel of beer connected to the one and only pump handle. He was wearing a collarless shirt and dungarees and looked as if he'd just walked in from the allotment.

He pulled a foaming pint glass, and I took it to the hard bench seat opposite the spluttering gas fire. He came across and wiped my table with a damp cloth, and sat down next to me.

'Well now, Mark lad, I suppose you're here to see Mr Carnaby?'

The question took me by surprise. 'How did you know?'

'There's a few of us not too 'appy about the 'ounding of us traders by Sir John, bloody-busy-body Drummond and his council, not 'appy at all. I had one of those planning fellas round here yesterday telling me t'old pub sign was breaking some law or t'other. Bloody ridiculous, it's been up there since t'old king died. Nigel is going to sort it out for us, mind you.'

We heard the latch click and into the bar stepped the small rotund figure of Nigel Carnaby.

'Are my ears burning?' he chuckled. In his loud check brown suit and yellow bow tie, and a small fat cigar stuck in his smiling face, he presented the image of a cartoon bookie at the races.

'I was just telling young Mark here that you're going to sort out t'council for us, Mr Carnaby.'

Bobby got up and pulled another pint. The little man sank a good half in one. Pausing for breath, he belched loudly and came and sat down opposite me. His dark beady eyes were shining with excitement.

'I take it it was your report in the *Times*? Where does the press stand on this issue?'

'I'm the impartial observer, Nigel, you know I don't take sides.'

He grinned at me. 'Aye, and my uncle Nat is Prime Minister.'

'Drummond claims he's doing it for the benefit of the town, I thought the Civic Society would welcome him tidying up the high street.'

He took another swig from his glass and wiped his mouth with the back of his hand. 'I've had a word with a dozen or so of the shopkeepers and everyone agrees that the council should be encouraging trade instead of burdening them with ridiculous regulations. Business is bad enough without Drummond and his thought-police adding to the problem.'

He picked up my empty glass. 'Same again?'

'No thanks, Nigel, I've an appointment in Burnthorpe this afternoon. I've got to be on my way.'

'Well, we're holding a meeting here tonight, early doors, will you be here?'

It sounded promising. 'I'll be there.'

Kevin Johnson's office, on the third floor of the *Clarion* building, was a spacious room and as his secretary ushered me in, Johnson, a heavy man with dark hair greying at the temples, rose from his desk and shaking my hand guided me to a large conference table at the other end of the room where he sat opposite me.

'Would you like some coffee or tea?'

I declined, too anxious to know what this was all about.

'OK Mark, I'll come straight to the point.' From inside his jacket he pulled out an opened brown envelope and handed it to me.

Puzzled, I took out the single sheet of paper and read the typed message which was short and very much to the point: 'Sir James Drummond is having an affair with a young girl.' It was undated and unsigned.

I handed it back to Johnson without comment.

'It was sent through the post to me at home. You know Drummond, what do you think, could it be true?'

'There is nothing new in sending an anonymous letter to a newspaper. It's probably a nasty prank, someone trying to make mischief.'

'Or an injured party seeking revenge,' he added.

'Well if that is the case, you could be sitting on one hell of a story. Who else knows about it?'

'Only you and Paul Winter.' Paul was the *Clarion's* editor.

'Why me?'

He leaned back in his chair and took off his dark horn-rimmed glasses. 'If this information were true, and I'm not suggesting for one moment that it is, but just supposing Drummond is having it away, what would you do if you were in Paul's shoes?'

I sat back and tried to be objective.

'If it is true, and the girl is under age, he would be committing an offence, but otherwise there is nothing illegal about having an affair.'

Johnson replaced his glasses. 'What about the moral stance? Drummond is perceived as a pillar of society, he's a magistrate, chairman of the council, holds high office in the Freemasons and is a very successful business man.'

'I would ask myself would our readers want to know about his extra-marital activities.'

'And?'

'The answer is, yes of course they would.'

Either Johnson was being extremely naive, or I was missing something. Paul Winter could have told him this without dragging me thirty miles out of my way.

'So are you saying, in your opinion, that we should investigate this letter?'

'Certainly.'

Johnson looked silently at the ceiling for a moment then, fastening his eyes on mine, said, 'And what if I told you that Drummond was one of the *Clarion's* major shareholders?'

This was news to me. Suddenly Johnson's problem came sharply into focus.

'You do see my predicament, Mark?'

I nodded. 'If the story gets out, and the *Clarion* hasn't covered it, it looks like an attempted cover up. On the other hand if you investigate Drummond and publish, it could have significant repercussions on career prospects.' I was now one step ahead of his game plan. 'So you want me, Mark Devlin freelance of this parish, to handle the hot potato? I break the story first in the nationals, then the *Clarion* can follow it up in all innocence. Thereafter, the *Clarion* staff cannot then be accused by your board of instigating a witch hunt against one of your influential colleagues.'

He smiled broadly. 'You have it in one, Mark. As long as we do not break the story first, no one can seriously complain.' Rising, he offered his hand. 'I'm so glad we understand each other. Call in on Paul before you go, he's expecting you. Oh, incidentally . . .'

I paused at the door as he tapped the letter.

'I've checked it out, Drummond has been seen with a young woman in Mallingborough.'

Down on the first floor I almost bumped into Paul Winter coming out of the gents' washroom.

'I take it he's put you in the picture?' he grinned.

'He's a bit of a devious bugger, isn't he?'

'What do you think?'

'If what he says is true, then my advice is batten down the hatches. I wouldn't want to be around here when the tabloid proverbial hits the fan. If I'm going to handle this, I'll need someone to follow Drummond. Harry Gorton will do it, he's always looking for extra cash. Talking of which . . .'

Winter put up his hands. 'Don't worry, I'm tapping the MD's budget for this one.'

By the time I got back to the Three Jugs the place was heaving with noisy shopkeepers and I could just make out Carnaby's head in the centre of the mêlée. He was trying to address the assembly but no one was taking a blind bit of notice until

Bobby Watson pushed his way through with a couple of empty beer crates for their champion to stand on.

'Now you lot,' roared Bobby. 'Let's have a bit of order for Mr Carnaby.'

Gradually the traders fell silent as Carnaby, his yellow bow tie slightly askew clambered onto his rostrum.

'Ladies and Gentlemen, we are here tonight to discuss the council's, and in particular, Sir James Drummond's unreasonable attitude to the traders in this town. We can only succeed in defeating these council despots if all of us, and I mean all, stick together.'

'Aye that's right,' shouted Alfie Horton. 'All for one and one for all.'

Another loud beery cheer went up and I wondered just how long this lot had been here.

Carnaby started inspiring anarchy amongst his noisy followers, telling them to ignore the letters they would soon be receiving from the planning department, and urging them to ban all councillors and council officials from their shops.

'That's a bit drastic, Nigel,' shouted Eric Hutchinson who owned the bakery. 'We'll be cutting off our noses to spite our faces.'

But he was the only dissenter, the rest were all in favour and cheered Nigel to the rafters and Bobby Watson was pressed into serving more beer as the decibels rose. I indicated to Ted Bolton the town's young chemist, and John Hardcastle the local café owner, that we should step outside, and in the draughty corridor I asked them for their reaction to Drummond and his officials.

Hardcastle was incensed. 'For the past couple of years we have been intimidated by these vindictive pettyfogging regulations. First it is the council's zealous hygiene gestapo who are trying to put us out of business with their absurd and oppressive legislation, now it's Drummond and his planners. Well I say enough is enough, it's time we took a stand.'

Ted Bolton nodded emphatically. 'Absolutely right. They

invent these directives on the premise the public and the environment needs protecting, but their real aim is to try and control us and make life increasingly difficult. We have more listed buildings and conservation areas around here than anywhere else in the country.'

'What about banning councillors from your shop?' I asked him.

'I'm all for it, if it highlights our case.'

'But surely you will lose out financially?'

'Hardly. We are only talking about a handful of councillors, and it will be nothing compared to the inconvenience they'll suffer.'

'Can a chemist refuse to provide a prescription?'

'If I don't have it in stock, I can't supply it, can I?' he asked innocently.

Back inside the bar, Charlie Hardcastle the local printer, whose flagpole and new sign would have to come down under Drummond's new order, was agreeing to print 'Councillors are Banned' notices. Others were organising petitions, and generally I got the impression that if Guy Fawkes had been around, the Bridgefield insurgents would have welcomed him with open arms.

The story was now a natural for the tabloids and I spent a busy evening writing and filing my copy. I tried to contact Drummond for his side of the story, but he declined to come to the phone.

The following morning all hell broke out. It started with a telephone call from a jubilant Carnaby at seven o'clock.

'Get yourself and a photographer down here,' he chortled. 'And don't bother to contact the TV boys or local radio, I've already been in touch with them.'

'What's going on?'

'See you in the high street.'

Half an hour later as I turned into the high street, I couldn't believe what I was seeing. The twelve, giant multi-coloured, fibreglass donkeys, similar to those found on fairground roundabouts, had each been fastened outrageously at right angles to the brickwork above the shop fascias, their comical faces and baleful eyes looking down on the pavement in such a farcical manner I found myself laughing out loud.

Carnaby and a group of traders were laughing and joking on the pavement. 'Well, what do you think?' he asked, almost beside himself with excitement.

I shook my head in disbelieve. 'Where the hell did they come from?'

'I got them cheap from a pal of mine who has a scrapyard in Ellerthorpe. We collected them after the meeting.'

'Are they safe?' I asked, aware of the strong winds that blow down the street.

'Safe as houses,' declared Henry Childs who owned the ironmongers shop, and who had supplied the necessary fasteners and with Carnaby and his chums, had worked throughout the night putting the donkeys in position.

I just couldn't wait to see Drummond's face, when he saw them.

The tabloids had angled the story on the traders' decision to ban councillors from their shops, and the street began to fill with more and more sightseers as word spread. By nine o'clock I had enough quotes to fill a book. The majority of people I spoke to thought it was a marvellous joke, but I guessed it wasn't one shared by a couple of grim-faced officials who arrived from the council planning office and stood some distance away taking notes.

By lunch-time the story had spread like a bush fire, everyone it seemed wanted to see the Bridgefield donkeys, and further encouraged by the coverage on all the local TV and radio stations, the street was now packed with hundreds of visitors and the traders were reporting tremendous business.

'The man's a genius,' grinned Eric Hutchinson at the bakery, referring to Carnaby who at that moment was standing outside his shop giving yet another interview.

Harry Gorton thought it was his birthday. He had responded

to my urgent telephone call to abandon the Drummond trail and get over here. He hadn't taken much persuasion. Every national newspaper was ordering pictures from him, and in any case, it appeared Drummond was either out of town, or he had gone to ground. Throughout the day I tried desperately to get hold of him, but without success.

I had more luck with the Chief Planning Officer, Edward Woodhouse, who to his credit saw the funny side despite Carnaby and his pals making him and his department a complete laughing stock.

He insisted that the donkeys would have to come down, though.

'What happens if the traders refuse?' I asked.

'In that case we will have to serve enforcement orders.'

'And if the traders decide to go to appeal . . .?'

He sighed wearily. Paid officials don't readily criticise their chairmen, but I got the distinct feeling he resented Drummond for landing him in this mess.

'Well, if they appeal, it then goes up the line to the Secretary of State who will then appoint an inspector to hold twelve enquiries . . . each shop with a donkey.'

'But that could take years.'

'Let's hope they see sense before then.'

With Drummond unavailable, I had to rely on the council's PR department for quotes, and a pleasant young man, obviously under orders from above, gave me the usual non-committal guff about the council's responsibilities and the need to exercise a sensitive planning programme. No he had no idea where Sir James was, and no, he had no idea when next he would be in the building.

Jill's day off, of course, had been almost ruined by the number of telephone calls she had taken from the nationals, all anxious for me to keep them abreast of the story. That evening she insisted we returned to Bridgefield so she could see for herself what all the fuss was about.

The high street had taken on something of a carnival air.

Carnaby had urged the traders to keep their shop lights on and this additional illumination caused eerie shadows to form on the grotesque donkeys transforming them into huge ghoulish demons. Two jokers had found a pantomime horse and were parading up and down inside the costume, and groups of teenage girls squealed with delight when it chased them trying to nip their legs. It appeared that everyone in Bridgefield who owned a camera was out snapping the scene.

The following morning the high street donkeys stared out of every national newspaper. Some of the captions to Harry's pictures were quite hilarious and over breakfast Jill and I chortled at the treatment the subs had given the story. 'Council gets kicked up the ass' proclaimed one headline, and clever variations on this theme had been humorously adopted by most of the tabloids. Some of the broadsheets actually included the story in tongue-in-cheek editorials, suggesting officials everywhere should heed the lesson coming from Bridgefield, especially in the light of the increased trade the donkeys were bringing to the town, and arguing that it would have been more to the economic point if Bridgefield planning department had thought of installing the donkeys in the first place.

The story had now made national TV and radio news, and by the end of the week, Bridgefield was staggering under its newly acquired notoriety and smiling shopkeepers were hardly managing to cope with the influx of visitors curious to see Carnaby's display. The man himself, confident that he now had the nation on his side, had arranged for an electrical firm to illuminate the donkeys. The high street was fast being transformed into a national shrine.

Harry Gorton and I were making a mint, selling stories to every conceivable outlet, including three foreign magazines. But by the end of the week, infuriatingly, there was still no sign of Drummond. The council PR department continued to field my questions patiently but insisted that Sir James was still out of town on business, and no, they had no idea where he had gone.

Two days later we got the break we needed. I could detect Harry's excitement as I answered the phone shortly before lunch-time.

'I've found him,' he announced triumphantly. 'And he *is* seeing a young woman.'

As ever, in situations like this, luck had played a major part. Harry had been sending off his pictures at Burnthorpe railway station around teatime the previous day, when the London train had pulled in, and among the passengers alighting was Sir James Drummond.

'I watched him collect his car from the car park himself, which I thought was a bit odd, because you had told me he was usually chauffeur driven. Anyway I followed him out of the concourse and I expected him to turn right onto the Bridgefield road but instead, he turned left, so I followed.'

'And?'

'I trailed his Rolls-Royce to Mallingborough where he pulled into the car park of the Crown Hotel. A few minutes later this car pulls up almost along side me. I didn't take much notice of the girl at the wheel until she got out and went over to Drummond's car. But I did get a shot of her getting into the car and Drummond leaning over and kissing her.'

'Good man. Then what?'

'A few minutes later they got out and went into the hotel. There were quite a few people milling about the reception area, and posing as a snap-happy tourist, I managed to get shots of her collecting a key, and more pictures of them going upstairs.'

'Brilliant. How long were they up there?'

'A good two hours, and when they finally did reappear, I followed them back to the car park, where they sat close together talking earnestly, his arm around her shoulder. When she finally got out, he leaned over and kissed her again.'

It all sounded highly suspicious and Harry agreed to come over with the pics straight away. Whilst I was waiting for him I telephoned the Drummond home yet again. A young man's voice answered, I knew Drummond had two sons. The eldest, Henry, was about fourteen. I took a chance.

'Can I speak to your father, Henry?' I tried to make it sound very matter-of-fact.

'It's Michael, actually,' replied the cultured voice of his younger brother. 'I'm afraid Father is not at home, and I have no idea when he will be back. Can I take a message?'

I told him I would try again later.

Harry's pictures were spot on. He'd captured the smiling girl in a mini skirt and an open-necked blouse, getting into Drummond's car, both smiling, with Drummond leaning over to kiss her.

'How old do you reckon, Harry?'

'I would say about twenty, twenty-one. She's quite a dish isn't she?'

I agreed.

'Time Sir James and I had a little chat, don't you think?'

'Rather you than me, old sport. I've still got some shots to take in Bridgefield. I'll check in with you later.'

Harry left me two sets of prints, and when he had gone I put one in a large envelope with my business card, on which I wrote, 'These have been brought to my notice. Can we talk?' I then melted some old sealing wax and with it secured the flap. On the front I wrote, 'Private and confidential, for the personal attention of Sir James Drummond', and fifteen minutes later I was turning into the Manor drive.

The Manor was a large four-square building in natural stone, and as I pulled up in front of the main entrance, I noticed, tucked away between two outbuildings, a silver grey Rolls-Royce. My arrival was being heralded by two barking dogs and as I rang the bell I heard a woman's voice commanding them to be quiet.

Like her husband, Lady Drummond was in her late forties, and was still a stunning looking woman, tall, slim with natural blonde hair which was pulled back from her face and secured at the back with an elastic band. Yet she was not a happy looking woman, in fact her face was like thunder as she looked down at me.

'Yes?' she asked imperiously.

I handed her the envelope. 'I have a special delivery for Sir James, and I'm instructed to await his reply.'

'From whom?' she demanded.

'The *Clarion* newspaper group.' I replied and watched her turn the envelope in her hands frowning at the seal.

'Sir James is not at home,' she announced abruptly. 'I'll see he gets it when he returns.'

I had been back in the house only ten minutes when he rang.

'Thank you for the parcel Mr Devlin. I found the contents most interesting.' His voice was slow and calm. 'Can I ask how they came to be in your possession?'

'Someone obviously thought I would be interested in them.'

He affected a tone of humorous surprise. 'Really?'

'Look,' I said, 'I would much rather we talked about this face to face.'

There was a long pause, then he said quietly, 'Right, nine thirty, here, in the morning.'

As soon as he had put the phone down I rang Paul Winter at the *Clarion* and alerted him to the fact that I could be breaking the story at the weekend in the Sunday tabloids.

'OK. But remember we haven't had this conversation,' he warned.

When Harry rang later he was almost jumping up and down with excitement when I told him what had happened. I couldn't blame him, we both knew the Sunday sleaze would pay handsomely for his Drummond pictures.

Drummond was surprisingly relaxed as he ushered me into his oak panelled study and beckoned me to sit on one of the two facing settees in front of a large fireplace. He sat down opposite, and leaning back comfortably, he crossed his legs and making a steeple with his fingers, tapped his lips thoughtfully.

'I understand you are the local freelance?'

'That's right.'

'So you are the man we must thank for putting Bridgefield under the national spotlight. I must congratulate you, you did a very professional job.' He smiled and nodded appreciatively.

'I'm not here to talk about Bridgefield, Sir James.'

He smiled broadly. He rose and going across to his desk, picked up the envelope I had delivered the previous day, and taking out Harry's pictures, handed them to me. 'You'll be wanting these back I suppose. Or do you have copies? Yes, of course you will have copies.'

He settled back into his seat.

'So you think I'm having an affair with this young lady?'

I held up the pictures. 'You've got to admit these look pretty incriminating.'

'This will come as a disappointment for you, Mr Devlin, but this young lady and I are just very good friends.' He saw me smile. 'A hackneyed phrase I agree, but true nonetheless.' He smiled and leaned back confidently into his seat again.

'So who is she?'

'And why may I ask, is that any business of yours?'

He didn't pose the question in an adversarial manner, but rather in such polite tones that I had the feeling I was suddenly skating on thin ice. I decided to take the gloves off.

'Look Sir James, it's not just a question of these pictures, I have also received a letter.'

'Ah, an incriminating anonymous note.' I had the distinct feeling he was now having a quiet laugh at my expense. 'And I suppose this letter suggested I was playing away from home.'

'It claims you and this woman are having a relationship.'

'It *was* anonymous?'

'Yes.'

He paused, then looked hard at me. 'So perhaps I should tell you, who sent it.'

I could feel the ice beginning to creak under my feet.

'You mean you know about the letter?'

'Let's say I can make a very good guess.'

I was becoming uneasy. Apart from myself and Harry, I had reckoned on only two other people knowing of the letter's existence and they were Kevin Johnson and Paul Winter. So just who was Drummond alluding to?

He was enjoying my obvious discomfiture.

'This is off the record. OK?'

'OK,' I agreed.

'Two years ago, I owned a publishing company in the Midlands. My chief executive at that time was found, shall we say, not to have the company's best interest at heart. I could have prosecuted him, but instead I sacked him, even gave him a reference, of sorts. In recent months, I have become involved in the *Clarion* group of newspapers, and shortly, there will be an announcement that I am taking over as chairman, in fact I've been in London this week, tying up the loose ends. Now,' He leaned forward conspiratorially, 'who do I find running the ship at the *Clarion*?'

'Kevin Johnson,' I replied.

'The very same Mr Johnson with whom I had that very serious altercation. It is no secret that I intend making a number of changes when I take charge, and I'll give you one guess as to what the first change will be.'

I took a deep breath. 'You are saying that Johnson wrote that letter himself, and then involved Paul Winter and me to expose you, to compromise your position at the *Clarion*, and so help him keep his job?'

'He's a conniving troublemaker, Mr Devlin. He knew an experienced freelance like you wouldn't rest until you had exposed my infidelity.'

'It doesn't explain these pictures.'

'Are we still off the record?'

I nodded.

'The woman you refer to happens to be my daughter, by my first marriage. She was only five when I was divorced, and soon after that she went to live with my first wife in Australia.

Twelve months ago she returned to this country, and decided she wanted to find me again.'

'So why the clandestine meetings?'

He grimaced and scratched his head. 'Not clandestine. Let's say expedient. Lady Drummond wasn't over-keen on the reconciliation, and in fairness, neither she nor Susie, that's my daughter, saw eye to eye. So to avoid unpleasantness we meet away from here. Susie's company occasionally sends her up North, and we try to meet up when we can. It works out much better for everyone concerned this way. And it was on one of our occasional meetings that we had the misfortune to bump into Johnson in Ellerthorpe. You can imagine the old-fashioned look he gave me. But you see, Mr Devlin, it is not much of a story, and I would deem it a favour if you would just drop it.'

I knew as I sat there listening to this tall, forthright man, that he was telling the truth, there was no scandal. And he was right, there was no longer a story.

Harry was incandescent, when I told him.

'He's got to be lying,' he fumed. 'What were they doing in the hotel bedroom?'

'Actually they were having afternoon tea in his daughter's room, and there's no law against that.'

'And you believe that?'

'Yes I do. He may be arrogant and autocratic, but I don't think he's a liar.'

'I think he's twisted you round his little finger,' he scoffed.

'I'm sorry Harry, the story just doesn't stand up.'

'The gossip columns will buy a Sir-James-Drummond's-secret-assignation piece.'

I shook my head. 'No Harry, we would need cooperation for that, and in any case I've promised we'll drop it.'

'Like hell we will. I've put a lot of effort into this, Mark, I'm not going to waste those shots.'

I told Jill about Harry's reaction. 'What happens now?' she asked.

'I'm not quite sure,' I replied.

Harry and I had cooperated well as a freelance team ever since we had both been made redundant from the *Clarion*, but I had no control over him. Like me, he was an independent who could do his own thing. If he decided to sell his pictures, and drop me in it with Drummond, there was nothing I could do about it.

My fears were further heightened that evening when Carnaby called me from the Three Jugs.

'Your Harry Gorton has just sold me some very interesting pictures of my friend Drummond. Very damning,' he announced triumphantly.

I groaned inwardly. What the hell was Harry up to?

'Is Harry still there, Nigel? Can I speak to him?'

'I very much doubt he could talk to anyone. Is it true that your mate drinks for England?'

'Look Nigel, there are a few things you ought to know about those pictures. Hang on in the Jugs. I'll be there in ten minutes.'

As usual he was holding forth at the bar as I entered the pub. When he saw me he moved to an empty table and I took my drink and joined him.

'Nigel, about these Drummond pictures . . .'

But before I could continue, he put a hand on my arm, and stopped me in my tracks. From his inside pocket he took out the envelope containing Harry's pictures and laid them on the table.

'Listen Mark, I might be a cocky arrogant little bugger, but I'm not into this sort of thing. These pictures look very incriminating, but they've got nothing to do with me. What Drummond does in his private life is his business.'

'It's not what you are thinking, Nigel. These pictures are . . .'

Again he interrupted me. 'Mark, I don't want to know.'

Suddenly I was seeing a new side to Nigel Carnaby, and I was further taken aback when he put the pictures back inside his jacket and said, 'I'll see Drummond gets these, he'll rest easier if he destroys them himself.'

The following morning Drummond rang me.

'I thought you would be interested to know that I've given instructions to the council's PR department to issue a press statement later this morning. I think we might have misjudged this fellow Carnaby.'

My story on how Drummond and the Chief Planning Officer were having a change of heart over the high street row hit the streets the following morning. It amounted to a complete climb down by the planning department with Drummond saying he hoped to meet Mr Carnaby to discuss the traders' problems.

'A most enterprising advocate for Bridgefield,' he added.

'Bloody hell,' chortled Carnaby after he'd seen the story. 'How did you manage to get that out of him?'

'Perhaps it was a token of gratitude. His way of saying thank you.'

He roared with laughter. 'I tell you what Mark, if he's going to be that generous I might just let him have the rest of the negatives.'

He was joking, I think.

Flight of Fancy

As I pulled up in front of the row of terraced cottages in the centre of Sessington, the small energetic figure of Elsie Hardcastle emerged, and bustling down the path she greeted me enthusiastically.

'It's lovely to see you again, Mark. Come on in.'

I kissed her on the cheek, and following her back to the cottage, I stepped into the small living-room, marvelling as always at the time warp it represented. The room was exactly as I remembered it as a young lad, the old table was still under the window, with its same green cover, trimmed with a fringe of velvet bobbles. 'Uncle' Charlie's well-polished rocking chair was still in evidence by the gleaming black fire range where the kettle was on the boil. The only modern intrusion as far as I could see was the colour TV which stood next to the grandfather clock ticking away in the corner.

I reckoned Elsie had been living here for close on sixty years, which made her around eighty-five. Before my parents died, Elsie and my mother had been great friends, but she and I had lost touch when I went to work in London. Since my return however I occasionally called in on her.

'Pull up the rocking chair Mark, and make yourself comfortable, kettle's just about boiled.'

She took down the old enamel tea caddie from its place on the mantelshelf and began fussing with the teapot.

'Well Elsie, what's the problem? Jill tells me you sounded rather mysterious when you telephoned.'

She handed me my tea and sat down on a hard-backed chair, her pale blue eyes sparkling with excitement as she smoothed her skirt.

'I'm getting married,' she announced, and laughed self-consciously as she saw my raised eyebrows. 'Are you shocked?' I grinned at her. 'Not in the least. I'm very happy for you. Who is the lucky fellow?'

'Tommy Fortnight.'

My journalist's brain cells leapt into action. Tommy Fortnight was nearly ninety.

'Eighty-nine, to be exact,' said Elsie reading my thoughts. 'Do you think I'm too young for him?' she giggled. 'He asked me two days ago, and the more I thought about it, the more sense it made. I look at this this way, Mark: he lives three doors away and ever since Rachael died, I've kept an eye on him, seeing to his washing, and making sure he is getting the right things to eat. Every day I am backwards and forwards running after him, if nothing else, it'll save my legs if he moves in here.'

Everyone in the village knew Tommy Fortnight. He had worked with Charlie on the Bridgefield railway all his working life, and for most of that he had driven his steam engine on a fortnightly journey to and from a timber yard on the coast, and had picked up the nickname as a result.

He was still a tough little character and it was impossible to believe this former amateur lightweight boxing champion was such a good age. He remained a handsome chap, with a head of thick white curly hair, and with his small wiry frame and sprightly gait, looked more like a man in his seventies. Every morning, in all weathers, he could be seen striding out to the newsagents, smartly swinging his walking stick, and prepared to stop and chat with anyone with the patience to put up with his deafness. Without his hearing aid, Tommy was as deaf as a post, which meant any conversation was invariably reduced to a few words bawled into his ear.

'So when is the big day?'

'Next Tuesday, at Bridgefield registry office. It will be just a quiet affair, but I want you and Jill to come.'

'We'd be delighted. But what am I doing here now?'

'Well, I want to give him a special wedding present, but I don't know whether it's possible or not, that's why I need to talk to you. You know about these things.'

'What things?' I asked, accepting one of her home-made scones.

'Those glider things you fly around in over Scar Top.'

'Gliders?'

'That's right, gliders. He wants to go up in one.'

'You're kidding.'

She shook her head. 'No I'm serious, he's always wanted to go up in one of those contraptions. I thought if it could be arranged, and it wasn't too expensive, I would give it to him as a wedding present. You do still fly up there?'

'Yes I do, but I'm not sure this is a good idea.'

'Why not?'

'I know Tommy is a hard little customer, but gliding is hardly the sport for an eighty-nine-year-old. It's not like getting into a comfortable airliner, you know.'

'You know Tommy, Mark, he's always refused to accept his age, and apart from his deafness he's still fit as a lop. Anyway he wouldn't have to do anything energetic, he would just sit there and enjoy it. Go on, say you'll do it, please take him up.'

I knew it would make a great story, but I wasn't going to be pressed into an answer before I had discussed it with Jimmy Garbutt, the club's flying instructor.

'You don't know what it will mean to him. Have another scone.'

'No thanks Elsie, I must dash.' I got up and kissed her on the cheek. 'I'll promise to think about it. I'll get back to you tomorrow.'

Jimmy Garbutt wasn't particularly worried when I telephoned

him for his advice. 'If he's fit, and you pick the right day, I can't see any reason why he shouldn't go up.'

Elsie rang me early the following morning wanting to know if she could go ahead and tell Tommy about his wedding present, and although I still had niggling doubts, I finally agreed to take him up the following Sunday, providing the weather was favourable.

'Eh, Mark, thank you, that's wonderful.' Then more seriously, 'Now, how much is it going to cost?'

'A photograph of you and Tommy standing next to the glider.'

'You mean for the papers. Oh, Tommy will love that, I'll go round now and tell him.'

'Hang on Elsie, I need to be in on this. We'll go together this afternoon.'

When Tommy opened the door to us it was Elsie who took over.

'Now Tommy Fortnight,' she announced, 'switch on that hearing aid of yours, I have no intention of bawling and shouting what I have got to say.'

The little man grinned at her and adjusted his ear piece. 'This is Mark Devlin, he works for the *Weekly Times*, and he is a glider pilot.'

I watched the old man's eyes light up as Elsie explained what she had been up to. 'Eee lad, that's grand,' he said. 'When do we start?'

'Sunday morning if the weather is right. I'll collect you and Elsie. You'll need to wear warm clothing, it can be a bit chilly up there.'

'So see you put your long johns on,' Elsie ordered.

I explained how I wanted to run the story for the papers and have photographs taken of him and Elsie, and he was all for it. I spent a further useful fifteen minutes listening to his life history and finally left him and Elsie to sort out his clothing for the flight.

The tabloids were particularly interested in Elsie and Tommy when I rang round the various news desks with the idea. Tom Hall at the *Clarion* readily agreed to having Harry Gorton airborne to take air-to-air shots of Tommy aloft with me.

'Incidentally Mark, has Paul Winter been in touch today?'

'Not that I know of, but I've been out most of the time. Why?'

'Hang on. I'll try and raise him.'

'Do you want the bad news, or the bad news,' said Paul when he came on the line.

I groaned.

'Go on.'

'Sir James Drummond?'

'What about him?'

'You know he's now our new chairman. Well, the new chairman had got a niece, who rejoices in the name of Constance Barnaby-Payne.'

'Paul I'm in a hurry, is this relevant?'

'Very relevant.' His emphasis was on both words. 'Constance has just completed her training course on one of Drummond's papers in the Midlands, and she is joining us as a reporter. Sir James wants her to get experience in the field, and he has suggested we attach her to you for three months. From your point of view it's not a bad idea, because she should help you to increase your output, at no extra cost, because the *Clarion* will still be paying her salary.'

'Do I have any choice?'

'Not if you want to keep on the right side of Drummond.'

'And why should I want to do that?'

'You never know,' he added mysteriously.

I could see Jill wasn't at all sure about the arrangement when I told her over supper that night. 'Why you? Why not one of the *Clarion* staff reporters?'

'It seems Sir James thinks she should be trained only by the best.'

'You are a conceited oaf. Where is she going to stay?'

'It's all in hand. She's got digs at the White Hart.'

'When does Miss Constance arrive. I take it, she is a Miss?'

'Tomorrow morning, nine o'clock sharp. She can start by making the police calls.'

The following morning I was just about to ring Jim Slater at the White Hart to check if my new assistant had arrived, when she beat me to it.

Her voice was refined, with a hint of humour in it. 'Hello Mark, it's Constance Barnaby-Payne. What time do I start?'

'Right now,' I replied briskly. 'Do the police, fire and ambulance calls, then get round here and we'll talk.'

'I've already done them.'

She waited for my response to this piece of initiative.

'And?' I asked.

'All's quiet on the Western front, sir.'

It took her ten minutes to walk from the White Hart.

'OK, I'll get it,' Jill announced as the doorbell rang.

'I thought you might,' I smiled.

Constance had done her homework. 'You must be Jill,' I heard her say. 'I'm Constance Barnaby-Payne, I'm your partner's new assistant.'

Jill led her into the small back room I use as a study, and as she introduced me, I gazed into the clear blue eyes of Drummond's niece. Later I was to describe her over the phone to Harry Gorton as tall, with short blonde hair, blue eyes, and a warning that if he stepped out of line, she would eat him for breakfast. But right now I could only stare as she greeted me with a stunning cheery smile.

'I'll leave you two to get acquainted,' said Jill closing the door, at the same time throwing me a look that said, I'll be keeping an eye on you matey.

Constance flopped into an armchair, and crossing her long legs, grinned at me.

'I've heard a lot about you,' she announced.

I held her gaze. 'You mean you've heard I'm a brilliant handsome reporter, with an incisive wit and acerbic turn of phrase that strikes fear into those who tread the corridors of power. Right?'

'Something like that,' she laughed.

'And you are the nineteen-year-old niece of one of our leading citizens, who after leaving your red brick university with a third-rate media studies degree, walked straight into a job on the *Sentinal* because it just so happened your dear uncle owned the paper.'

Her smile vanished and I saw her bristle at my suggestion. 'That's not fair.'

'Isn't it? Then you'd better start proving otherwise, fast.'

I held up a blank piece of copy paper. 'Do you know what this is?'

I suppose I expected her to respond with a stare as blank as the paper itself. Instead her voice hardened.

'It's your meal ticket, you are a freelance, not only do you have to put words down on that paper, you've got to sell them to someone prepared to pay good money for them. OK?'

I sat back and viewed Miss Constance in a new light.

'Look Mark, I'm no dummy, I know how hard a freelance has to grind out a living. I had a boyfriend in the business, he worked so hard we hardly saw each other. But you're right, there are those at the *Clarion* who will think just like you, and view this job as sheer nepotism, especially after all the redundancies last year. That's why I jumped at the chance of working with someone like you to get some real experience under my belt.'

'All right,' I said quietly. 'Let's start defining some ground rules.'

For the next hour she sat and listened quietly while I explained how I worked the district. We agreed that for the first two weeks she would accompany me on jobs, and after that, she would take on certain responsibilities of her own. She would use her room at the White Hart as her office, and make whatever arrangements were necessary with Jim Slater for the use of his phone, and we agreed that time off would be by mutual agreement.

As we came to the end, she smiled at me. 'Can I ask a favour? Please don't call me Constance. All my friends call me Connie.'

I brought her up to date on the stories in the diary, and she was particularly impressed with Tommy Fortnight's forthcoming wedding and Elsie's special wedding present.

For the rest of the day, with Connie at the wheel of her old Ford Anglia, I accompanied her on a tour of the area. At lunchtime I took her into the Three Jugs where she startled Bobby Watson by ordering a pint of his best bitter, and then raised a few eyebrows when I introduced her to some of my contacts at the Bridgefield nick. That evening Jill and I walked over to the White Hart and found her the centre of attention.

'I bet she never has to buy a drink in here,' Jill observed, as Connie came across pint glass in hand, and joined us.

'Well, how did your first day go?' Jill asked her.

'Exciting. I'm looking forward to working with your fella.' Then, turning to me, 'I've done the calls. There's been a barn fire at Orton's farm, nothing serious. I've put a couple of pars over to the *Clarion*.'

'Right, tomorrow morning, I want you to go and interview Tommy Fortnight, get as much background as you can, we'll need it for the wedding story.'

Later, as we walked home Jill looked at me sideways. 'Do you find her attractive?'

'She's OK I suppose.'

She saw me smile, and dug me in the ribs with her elbow.

The Bridgefield Flying Club is perched 700 feet above the town on Scar Top Bank, a hill with a natural plateau from which the gliders are launched by winch.

The clubhouse is a spartan old Nissen hut obtained shortly after the last war, and after all these years it still retains that evocative dank smell well known to all servicemen. The casement windows rattle in the wind, and the screws in the door hinges are loose in the rotting frames and generally the building has been fighting a losing battle against the elements for years. But it provides a welcome refuge for members who use it to drink coffee and eat a quick sandwich between flights, or sit on the old three piece suite with its stuffing sticking out of the armchairs, whiling the time away until weather conditions improve.

I couldn't have chosen a better day for Tommy's flight. As we approached the summit of Scar Top Bank with Jill at the wheel and Tommy and Elsie in the back of her jeep, I could see two gliders already aloft wheeling in search of the rising wind currents and drew them to the attention of a visibly excited Tommy, who craned his neck for a better view and pointed them out to Elsie.

Over her shoulder Jill shouted at him. 'Tommy, are you sure you want to go ahead with this, it's not too late to change your mind.'

He ignored her and Elsie turned to him. 'Tommy, Jill's talking to you.'

'Pardon?'

In exasperation, Elsie pointed to his ear, ordering him to switch on his hearing aid, which he did reluctantly. 'Why you keep switching the blessed thing off beats me,' she chided him.

'It picks up a lot of noise, can't always hear voices, gives me a headache at times.'

Jill parked the jeep on an open space next to the hangar, and Jimmy Garbutt came across from the clubhouse smiling and shouting his hellos. I leapt out and helped Tommy to the ground. Elsie was already out of the vehicle before Jill could offer her assistance.

Grasping Tommy's hand, Jimmy shook it enthusiastically. 'Tommy, it's a great pleasure meeting you. How are you feeling, young man?'

Tommy adjusted his hearing aid and smoothed his hair down

against the brisk wind. 'Champion young feller, right champion,' he grinned confidently.

'That's the spirit. Why don't we all go in the clubhouse and have a coffee while Mark gets things ready for you?'

As they disappeared I went over to the hangar where the tandem two-seater K13 was housed and found Peter Brack, a club veteran, tinkering with the air speed indicator.

'Problems?' I asked.

'I think a drop of water must have got in it, it was giving a false reading, but it's OK now.'

Behind me in a cloud of dust Connie pulled up and she and Harry Gorton got out. Harry I could see was not his usual cheery self.

'Mark, I'm not happy about this job I can tell you, I've never been up in one of these things before, and frankly I'm bloody scared stiff.' He viewed the K13 with deep hatred. 'You're not telling me these things can take two people up there.'

Peter Brack and I laughed at his discomfiture.

Connie reassured him. 'If an eighty-nine-year-old can do it, you shouldn't have any problems.'

He wasn't convinced. 'What height will we reach?'

'Around 1200 feet,' I said.

'That's higher than the Eiffel Tower,' he gasped.

'Look Harry, if you are really that worried about it, you can always duck out, there is no disgrace, lots of people change their mind at the last minute.'

He shook his head. 'Tom Hall would kill me if I didn't get this picture, anyway I wouldn't be able to live it down.'

'Come on,' I said, leading them towards the clubhouse. 'I'll introduce you to your pilot, and if it makes you feel any better, he's our chief flying instructor, the most experienced flyer in the club.'

I explained to Connie that Jimmy Garbutt would take Harry up in the club's other K13 ahead of Tommy and me, and keep his glider slightly higher and to one side to allow Harry to get shots of Tommy sitting in front of the cockpit. In the clubhouse we found Tommy laboriously signing the indemnity forms and Jill serving coffee from behind the small refreshment bar. I took Jimmy to one side and introduced Harry and warned him that he was feeling a little apprehensive.

Jimmy nodded understandably. 'First time up? Never fear. You'll love it once you are up there.'

Harry's white face suggested otherwise, and when Jimmy handed him what to the uninitiated looks like a rucksack with two hanging straps he glanced at me for an explanation.

'Your parachute,' I prompted.

'Parachute!' he croaked. 'Good God, Mark, I thought you said these things were safe.'

'Relax,' said Jimmy. 'You'll be more comfortable with it on. It will act as a cushion for your back.'

The launch point for the gliders was almost a quarter of a mile from the clubhouse at the end of an inclined track along which a tractor slowly hauled the unoccupied planes with helpers walking alongside, steadying the wings. I had arranged with Jimmy, against all regulations, to take Tommy up there in Jill's jeep.

Harry took pictures of Elsie giving him a big kiss in front of the glider and Connie took them back to wait in the jeep to watch Jimmy and Harry take off.

The wind was increasing and as I helped Harry into the front seat and checked his safety straps Jill pressed the nose of the glider down with one hand to prevent the wind lifting it, and with the other she steadied the open canopy. He was still looking whey faced as I handed him his camera gear, and as Jimmy clambered in behind him and started the pre-flight checks, I half expected him to chicken out.

Jill picked up a Day-Glo bat, and with an arm movement across her legs, signalled to the winch man to take up the slack. Jimmy put his thumb up, and Jill gave an overhead wave of the bat to the winch half a mile away. The next second the K13 was airborne.

I returned to the Jeep where Elsie had gone very quiet.

'You're sure it will be all right, Mark?' she whispered.

As if to answer her, Tommy opened the door and prepared to get out. 'Ehe that were grand, are we next?'

I nodded, and held the straps of his parachute pack open to allow him to get his arms through, then fastened up the straps between his spindly legs.

When Elsie saw what I was doing she became most concerned. 'He won't have to use that will he?' she gasped.

I assured her everything would be all right and with Tommy holding firmly onto Jill and I, he gingerly stepped onto the aluminium floorboards and gradually lowered himself into the small seat.

'Tommy,' I shouted. 'I'll be controlling the plane from the back seat, so don't touch this.' I tapped the control column between his legs, and placed his gnarled hands on the grab handle above the instrument panel.

Climbering in behind him, I checked the instruments and I was just about to close the canopy when Elsie came over and handed Tommy his inexpensive little camera. He grinned up at her, his eyes burning with excitement, and she bent down and planted a kiss on his cheek.

With the canopy closed and locked, I signalled for the tow wire to be attached and the slack taken up. I bent forward and shouted to Tommy that we were all set, but in that moment I noticed he had removed his hearing aid. We accelerated forward, bouncing on the uneven surface like a speedboat until we were dragged into a steep fifty-degree climb. At twelve hundred feet I dipped the nose and released the tow cable.

To the right and slightly above us, I could see Jimmy and Harry circling, and I made a gentle turn in their direction and together we flew an extended figure of eight making the most of the rising wind currents on the windward side of the hill ridge.

I could see Harry's camera lens glinting in the sunlight and I dipped the starboard wing to give him a better view of Tommy. I repeated the exercise two or three times until finally

Jimmy gave me the thumbs up and pointed to the ground indicating they had all the shots Harry needed, and they were landing. Jimmy made a steep turn over the runway and I watched him flick the K13 into the wind and point the nose steeply at the runway. I imagined Harry's face as he saw the ground rushing up towards him as Jimmy, with the finesse that befitted a chief flying instructor, pulled back on the stick holding the glider a few inches off the ground until the last moment before letting it sink gently onto the runway.

We had been aloft for five minutes, and I decided this was long enough for Tommy and I slipped the glider into a tight turn down wind. I knew immediately there were something wrong as we came out of the turn. The stick refused to respond to either a right or left hand movement. For a second I thought Tommy must have grasped the dual control stick in front of him, but as I glanced over his shoulder I could see he was still holding the grab handle on the nose.

I wrenched at the stick again. I had forward and backwards movement, but nothing sideways, and without aileron control I just couldn't turn the plane. With an increasing pulse rate, I tried to assess the situation calmly and logically. The altimeter told me we were still maintaining our launch height and I still had rudder control. Once again I battled with the stick, still no response.

I felt cold perspiration under my armpits, I knew I was now in serious trouble. We were flying in a straight line away from the airfield and unless a suitable landing area presented itself directly in front of us, the consequences didn't bear thinking about. To further complicate matters we were flying at a combined air and wind speed of 60 knots, and I knew of only one other pilot who had tried to put a glider down at that speed down wind. He had been crippled for life and his plane reduced to matchwood as it had ripped through a hedge and smashed into the side of a farm building.

On the ground Jimmy Garbutt would now be wondering why I was travelling so far down wind, and it would be only a matter of a few seconds before he realised I had problems. I imagined the hysterical repercussions this would create amongst the women standing there looking up at us. Meanwhile Tommy was sitting in front of me with two thumbs in the air blissfully unaware of the crisis going on behind his back.

We were now flying over the forest near Bardsey and the trees immediately produced a sinking effect on the plane and our height began dropping alarmingly. I estimated at this rate we had height and speed to travel only another mile or so. The trees also produced worrying turbulence, and without aileron control we began bouncing all over the place.

I wrenched at the stick once more, again the response was negative.

The forest passed under us to reveal a valley and a patchwork of fields separated by drystone walls. As we sped lower and lower, I searched desperately for a suitable landing area. The only possibility was a stubble field. The blocks of newly baled straw would prove fatal obstacles at this speed, but bales or not, my options had run out. I pushed the stick forward and applied the airbrakes but we were travelling far too fast down wind, and they had little effect on our rate of descent. I bellowed to Tommy to brace himself; if he heard me he didn't respond. Now we were crabbing away from the field. Desperately I banged hard on the rudder to try and straighten our course, and the glider responded by skidding sideways as if skating on ice.

We were now down to 200 feet and closing at a suicidal rate. I watched the hedgerows and trees rushing up towards us. It was then I saw the pylons. There was one either side of the field, and their high voltage cables were draped across our flight path. I estimated I had about 60–feet clearance at the most if I was to slip under them. I needed to lose more height, fast. A stone wall flashed beneath our nose and directly ahead was a stack of baled straw. I felt the tail skid clip it and the entire plane shuddered uncontrollably. The impact of landing at this speed would break the plane in two, but it was now or never.

I pulled back on the stick, and watched the perimeter wall rushing towards us. Pushing the stick forward I felt the single undercarriage wheel crash into the rough surface and we careered along bouncing like a demented kangaroo towards the wall. I banged on full rudder and saw the high voltage cables flash past overhead, but there was no avoiding the bales of straw stacked directly in our path, and the port wing smashed into them, whipping us around in a one-hundred-and-ninety-degree ground loop.

I sat there in the silence, listening to my heart pounding, trying to control my shaking limbs. Reaching out I unlocked the canopy and flung it back on its hinges and throwing off my straps scrambled out and felt a delicious cool breeze on my face. I was amazed to see the glider, although badly damaged, was still intact and further staggered to see Tommy calmly replacing his hearing aid.

As I released his straps he looked up at me grinning.

'That were grand – just like big dipper at Blackpool when I were a young fella'.' He looked around the field. 'Where's Elsie and Jill?'

His face was flushed and his eyes were shining with the excitement of the flight. He had been totally oblivious to the crisis and was obviously under the impression it had been a normal flight and we were back at the club.

'Are you OK?' I asked incredulously.

'Champion, right champion, I've always wanted to do that.'

I helped him upright and steadied him as he stepped out of the cockpit.

'Pity I couldn't take any pictures though.'

'Why didn't you?' I asked, helping him to sit down on one of the straw bales.

'Camera dropped off my knee when we turned, and I couldn't reach it.'

I looked into the front cockpit and felt my heart lurch. The camera had fallen in the space where the dual control stick comes up from the floor. Little wonder I had been unable to move it sideways, the camera had wedged it solid. I knew it was my fault, I should have insisted Tommy had worn it around his neck but I had been too distracted by the flight checks when Elsie had handed it to him. I tried to yank it away from the root of the stick, but then thought better of it. Jimmy would want to see it before he filed his report of the accident to the British Gliding Association. Suddenly I felt sick.

I felt dreadful. My limbs wouldn't stop shaking and despite the warm autumn sunshine my teeth were beginning to chatter uncontrollably.

'Airsickness?' Tommy enquired innocently.

'Something like that,' I replied, flopping down beside him.

'You need a drop of this,' he said, taking a silver hip flask from his pocket. 'Always keeps a little drop handy, good for the heart, so Doctor Hughes tells me.'

He took a swig and handed me the flask. I took a deep draught.

'Your camera's jammed. I'll have to get it out later.'

We watched the farm tractor and trailer bobbing towards us.

'Not very clever,' complained the driver as he pulled up in front of us, indicating with his outstretched arm the bales I had scattered with my forced landing. 'You frightened the bloody life out of me coming down like that. Do you realise you only just missed me?'

'I'm sorry about that. I'm afraid we ran out of air.'

I explained about Tommy's flight and Elsie's wedding present and finally introduced Tommy.

'Tommy Fortnight? Did you used to work on the railway?'

'Aye,' replied Tommy.

'You had a fireman called Billy Prentice.'

'Yer'right. Billy and me worked together for twenty years.'

'He was my old man. I'm pleased to meet you Tommy, he was always talking about you.'

'You must be young Terry, Billy's youngest.'

The middle-aged farmer laughed and nodded, and after that our untimely arrival in his field was quickly forgotten. Between us we hoisted Tommy onto the trailer and transported him to the farmhouse where Mrs Prentice put the kettle on and I telephoned the flying club.

It took Jimmy and his rescue vehicle almost an hour to reach us, and when they got out, Elsie was as white as a sheet and Jill was near to tears. We held each other tightly for a minute then, satisfied she had recovered her composure, I took her and Jimmy to one side and explained what had happened.

Jill was horrified, and immediately wanted to call an ambulance for Tommy.

'It's not necessary,' I assured her. 'He has no idea he's been in an emergency. He thinks that type of landing is quite normal, and he enjoyed every minute of it. I don't think we should tell him, or Elsie for that matter.'

Jimmy agreed, and Jill went across to Tommy who wide-eyed was chattering away telling Elsie and Mrs Prentice about his flying adventure. She cast a professional eye over him.

'No bumps or bruises Tommy?' she asked casually.

'Nay lass, gliders aren't like locomotives. Now shunting locos can knock 'ell out of you at times, if you'll pardon the expression.'

'Where's Connie?' I asked.

'She's gone with Harry to get shots of your glider.'

'Like hell she has,' I said, making for the door.

'It's a fantastic story, Mark,' Connie trilled when I caught up with them. 'And now it has got two new vital ingredients – drama and danger.'

Harry was busy working out camera angles. 'Come over here Mark and let me get a shot of you next to the wreck.'

'Listen, you two. There is no way we are using the crash landing.'

Connie was crestfallen and as usual Harry was bolshie.

'Why not?' he demanded. 'It's a perfect story, with a perfect ending.'

I sat down on one of the bales and explained how Tommy and Elsie were blissfully unaware of the emergency. 'Can you imagine the repercussions if they were to read what danger Tommy had been in?'

Reluctantly they agreed. But that night in the White Hart, Connie came down from her bedroom and handed me two sheets of copy. Glancing through the first paragraph I felt my anger rising as I began reading the Tommy and Elsie story. As a report it was very well done, full of dramatic incident, and very accurate. She hadn't missed a trick and had angled the ending to include a handsome courageous flyer and a tearful Elsie taking brave Tommy in her arms and, amid the wreckage, he asking her to marry him.

'Who have you given this to?' I demanded.

'Just about everyone, the tabloids, the broadsheets, everyone's taken it.'

I was just about to explode when I saw the start of her slow smile. Then she laughed. 'I'm sorry Mark, I couldn't help winding you up. Anyway I thought it would be good practice. What do you think of it?'

'It shows promise,' I admitted.

'Patronising bastard.'

'That,' I said decisively, 'is going to cost you a very large brandy.'

'You deserve one.'

Any hope Elsie had of keeping their wedding a quiet affair was out of the question. The Sessington bush fire had already spread the news and on Tuesday morning there were scores of bystanders outside the registry office to see the happy couple.

Connie and Harry were waiting there for them to emerge, and I gave Connie a couple of additional paragraphs on the ceremony to include in the 'soaring to happiness' story we had prepared earlier.

Jill and I were invited back to Elsie's where she had laid on a special tea and Harry and Connie came along later, after she had put her copy over and Harry had got his pics away.

'How did the ceremony go, Elsie?' Connie asked tucking into Elsie's cream sponge.

'Well dear, there was a nasty moment when Tommy here refused to answer the vows,' Elsie looked very serious.

'Really?' Connie was wide-eyed. 'What happened?'

'I gave him a sharp jab in the ribs, and he soon switched on his hearing aid,' she laughed.

Lilies at a Funeral

The gypsy caravans began arriving in Sessington that Sunday evening, hauled slowly up the main street towards the common by tired looking horses nodding against the strain of the incline. Bringing up the rear were small groups of four or five horses fastened by their halters to the tailboards, their broken steps adding a rhythmic counterpoint to that of the unseen leaders striving between the shafts ahead of them.

Sitting alongside me in the car parked on the grass verge, Connie counted at least fifty horses in the column.

'Look at her,' she cried in admiration, pointing to a striking golden palomino mare. 'Isn't she gorgeous?'

This was Connie's final week with me, and it was fitting it should coincide with the Sessington Easter Horse Fair, because I knew she was crazy about horses.

The fair was an annual fixture in Sessington's rural calendar. Originally it was conceived as a venue for the travellers to buy and sell their horses, but with the passing of time it had developed into a major gypsy rally. Some of the locals welcomed the influx of visitors and the additional trade they brought to the village, others, mindful of the increase in burglaries and violence that usually came with it, were less charitable.

Connie and I had spent the afternoon gathering just such opinions for the story she had filed with the *Clarion*, and most of the quotes we had from the villagers expressed concern and anxiety.

We waited until the last of the gypsies had passed, then

slipping the car into gear, I followed them to their site on the common where we. Watched the men, their trilby hats on the backs of their heads and coloured scarves round their necks, gather in groups around hastily built fires, as the womenfolk, their shawls pulled tightly round their shoulders against the cold of the evening, busied themselves preparing supper.

Connie wanted to see the palomino again but when she caught sight of the man attending the horse her eyes widened in awe.

'That's Big Tim the Gypsy,' I chuckled.

Her reaction had been similar to mine when I had first met him. He wasn't particularly tall, but he must have weighed in at about twenty stones. He had stretched a dirty T-shirt over his barrel chest and over this he wore an open dark leather waistcoat with two horse brasses pinned to it. His closely cropped hair and dark penetrating eyes added a menacing dimension to his imposing build.

'He's the gaffer,' I explained. 'The leader of the gypsies and in this part of the world, his word is law. No one defies Big Tim.'

'I can well believe it,' she exclaimed. 'Would you pick a fight with him?'

She got out of the car, wandered over and began stroking the palomino. Big Tim immediately appeared from behind his caravan and went across to her, walking with his arms slightly adrift from his body, as if the very act of walking was a constant balancing act. He inclined his head towards her on a neck as thick as a tree trunk. He really was enormous. I remembered the story of how single handed, he had hoisted a car off a trapped mechanic after the jack had slipped, and held it until the man was pulled free. I smiled to myself as I watched her set about charming him with that wonderful smile of hers, and within minutes they were both laughing aloud and Connie was teasing the horse's cream mane.

'He's something else,' she said when she came back to the

car. 'He actually won that horse in a bare-knuckle fight, she's
his pride and joy.'

She pointed to a tall well-built youth talking to Tim.

'That's his son, Ganton.' I told her. 'You should have a fiver
on him in the race tomorrow.'

I told her this race was as unofficial as it was illegal. 'It
originated, so the story goes, shortly after the war when a
young gypsy started shooting his mouth off about his horse,
which he claimed would beat all comers over a mile. The
challenge was accepted by the then leader of the gypsies, a
purse was agreed, and the race has been an established feature
of fair day ever since. At four o'clock every Easter Monday,
tradition requires the leader to choose the course for the race.
The only difference these days is that three gypsies take part.'

'How do they decide them?'

'Are you sitting comfortably?' I laughed, as I began to explain
the intricate selection process. 'It's a bit of an auction. One
of the gypsies will declare his horse to beat all comers, and
announces his purse of, let's say £10. This requires those wish-
ing to race against him to meet that purse.

'At this stage there are likely to be any number of contenders
who fancy their chances, and they all agree to match the purse
of £10. Now as long as there are more than three gypsies in
the bidding, the first one has to raise his original purse, let's
say to £20. Some of the challengers will drop out, but as long
as there are more than three remaining, the first gypsy has to
continue raising his stake, until only two challengers are left.'

'Where does all this bidding take place?'

'Around the leader's caravan, about an hour before the race.
Two years ago, the purse reached £275.'

Connie's eyes widened. 'That's £550 to the winner,' she
exclaimed. 'But isn't it dangerous, racing along a country lane,
what about the traffic?'

'They simply position a couple of wagons across the highway
at the start and at the finish, and block the section off. Obviously, the police aren't happy with this arrangement, but by the

time they get to know which course Tim has chosen the race is over, so they tend to turn a blind eye. I know they're concerned at the amount of side betting that goes on, either.'

'Does a lot of money change hands?'

'A hell of a lot, and bad losers can cause trouble, and remember these races are hardly governed by Jockey Club rules!'

Back at Bardsey, I dropped Connie off at the White Hart, and later that night when Jill and I joined her for a drink we found her in the bar looking thoughtful.

'Who's this bloke called Barry Chapel?' she asked, as I put a pint of beer in front of her, and gave Jill a gin and tonic.

'A bloody legend around these parts, that's what,' chipped in Jim from behind the bar. 'Don't you go messing with the likes of Chapel, lass.'

It was good advice.

'Standing at six foot six and built like a brick coal house, he was about thirty going on fifty five, with a face hewn from soft stone.'

'He's a real villain' I told her. 'Why do you ask?'

'About ten minutes ago I overhead a couple of blokes talking about the horse fair tomorrow, they mentioned this Barry Chapel, and I got the impression they were expecting him to cause some sort of trouble.'

'So what's new?' Jim scoffed. 'Trouble, is Chapel's middle name. He's been barred from every pub around these parts, including this one,' he added with feeling. 'Do you remember that Saturday night, Mark, when he drank nine pints of ale, and I told him he'd had enough.'

'What happened?' Connie demanded.

'He took on three coppers single-handed in the backyard and was only finally arrested when reinforcements arrived from Bridgefield.'

'Chapel caused a lot of trouble at the fair last year,' I told Connie. 'He had a fight with one of the gypsies which ended in Chapel sticking a knife into him.'

Jill turned to Connie. 'That's right. I was on duty when they brought him in. It was touch and go, he could easily have bled to death, and then we heard he'd died a couple of months after he was discharged.'

'What happened to Chapel?' Connie asked.

'Nothing,' I told her. 'The police tried their best to pin an attempted murder charge on him, but they never found the weapon and as usual there were no witnesses, at least no one willing to come forward, and the victim declined to name him.'

'Even as a youngster he was a violent little devil,' said Jim. 'Always terrorising the kids at school. Have you seen where he lives?'

'Not a pretty sight,' I agreed.

'Why, what's wrong with it?' Connie asked.

'Nothing if you happen to like a front garden that doubles as a scrap yard,' retorted Jim.

He was right. The front of Chapel's modest pre-war semi was littered with wrecked cars, tyres, boats, old washing machines, all sorts of junk. What he did with it was anyone's guess, because he spent most of his time, when he wasn't in jail, drinking beer with other unsavoury types in his tin-sheet garage. The council had told him to clear up the mess on numerous occasions, but somehow hadn't got round to enforcing the instruction, and not surprisingly opposition from his neighbours was muted.

'Well, if Chapel and his mob do turn up tomorrow, you and Connie watch yourselves, do you hear?' Jill warned.

Most of the Sessington residents to whom Connie and I had spoken earlier had laid the blame for last year's troubles firmly at the door of Barry Chapel and I empathised with this viewpoint, having watched Chapel and his mates drinking and picking fights with the travelling men. Following the stabbing incident, there were now well founded fears that a number of scores had to be settled.

Connie got up and went to the bar. 'It's my round, and have one for yourself, Jim,' she offered.

'Very kind of you lass,' he said smiling. 'You know, we're

going to miss that happy smiling face of yours. It's the end of the week you leave, isn't it?'

'Friday,' replied Connie balancing drinks back to the table.

'Cheers Connie,' said Jill. 'We'll miss you.'

The cherry blossom in the gardens and the daffodils along the river bank brought a touch of spring to Sessington that Easter Monday when Connie and I arrived in the village. The number of travellers seemed greater than ever, and many of them were already parading their horses over the common.

'There must be over a hundred horses at this fair,' Connie announced as we entered a crowded Bertha Sanderson's and ordered coffees from the harassed owner. The tiny shop was so crowded, there wasn't a spare table and we had to take our coffee outside and stand on the pavement. Ten minutes later Harry Gorton, his sandy hair flapping in the breeze, ambled his way towards us.

'Is it all right for Harry to take pics of Big Tim's caravan,' asked Connie. 'The hand painted panels are really something, it'll make a nice photo feature.'

'Sure, if Big Tim is agreeable.'

This was the third year I had covered the horse fair, and I was scratching around to find something new and fresh to write about. Perhaps Connie had a point featuring the traditional caravans would at least make a change from horses.

She handed me her coffee cup, and grabbing Harry by the arm, led him away through the crowd of gathering sightseers. I was about to re-enter the shop when I noticed the familiar figure of Edith Perth coming towards me.

'It's nice to see a friendly face amongst all these strangers,' I greeted her.

'Aye lad, but there's a face over there I'd rather not be seeing today.'

She nodded in the direction of a group of men standing at the edge of the common, next to an old platform lorry. They were talking earnestly, and standing head and shoulders above them all was the menacing figure of Barry Chapel holding the lead of an evil looking Rottweiler dog.

Dave Challenor, the shirtsleeved licensee of the Blue Cat in Sessington, was doing good business. He'd been open since nine o'clock and by mid morning the place was heaving with travellers all shouting to be heard over the din. I fought my way to the bar and ordered a beer from one of the casual helpers Dave had taken on for the day and stood with my back to the bar, listening to the gypsies arguing about the purse for the race that afternoon.

Dave grinned over at me as he held a tray of empty pint glasses under the beer pump and began pulling frothing ale into them.

'Another quiet morning, Dave.'

'I'm not complaining,' he laughed.

Sitting in the centre of the small room, poring over a clip-board I saw Ronnie Muir, the local bookie. He too, looked to be doing good business as I pushed my way towards him. When he saw me he grinned.

'Now Mark lad, what's your fancy? I'll give you 1/2 on Big Tim's lad Ganton, 2/1 Harry Brewer and 6/1 Tommy Boy in the big race.'

'You are all heart, Ronnie,' I laughed. 'The purses haven't been decided yet.'

He tapped his nose with his finger and grinned. 'Listen to your uncle Ronnie, Mark, never been wrong yet.'

Which was true. He kept his ears close to the ground did our Ronnie, and by lunch-time on race day, he knew all about the best horses, and more importantly, who had the money to up the purse.

'Big Tim's mare will win, she always does,' I suggested.

'Now don't you be too sure about that. I've just taken a ton on Tommy Boy nag to beat gaffer's palomino.'

If that were true, either someone had money to burn, or

they were very confident of Tommy Boy, not only making the race in the first place, but equally satisfied he could win it.

'So it's between Ganton, Harry Brewer and Tommy Boy?' I said.

Ronnie tapped his nose again. 'Wouldn't be at all surprised,' he grinned.

I finished my beer and went outside, just in time to see a worried looking Connie approaching.

'What's the matter, did Big Tim give you a flea in your ear?'

'It's the palomino. It's gone missing.'

'Missing! It can't go missing, it was tethered outside his caravan.'

'It happened while he was showing us the inside of the caravan. When we emerged she had disappeared. Boy, is he in one hell of a temper.'

'It can't have gone far, everyone knows Tim's palomino.'

We crossed over to the common where scores of horses and ponies were now eagerly grazing, while the travellers argued their way to a sale. Unwilling animals were dragged by their owners to be put through their paces and trotted up and down in front of the prospective buyers, then pulled to a halt while their legs were checked for soundness. If the sale was agreed, the deal was sealed by a spitting on palms and a slapping of hands.

We could hear Big Tim shouting and bawling to a group of gypsies in the distance.

'Have you found the mare yet?' Connie asked as we approached the big man.

But before he could reply, we became aware of a commotion down the main street. The palomino was careering towards us with a large black dog at its heels.

Big Tim shouted frantically to the nearby travellers.

'Stop her, stop her, try to turn her, cut her off.'

But the din of the shouting and the barking dog only intensified the horse's panic. She suddenly veered to the right across the common, and at a flat-out gallop, headed straight down to the river bank. Again and again Tim urged his men to stop her, and half a dozen of them, with Connie and Harry and I bringing up the rear, set off in pursuit. The terrified beast was approaching the river at such a pace she couldn't have pulled up if she wanted to. We stopped and watched in horror as she took off from the river bank. There was no way she was going to make it.

At any other point in the river the water was about ten feet deep, enough to allow her to swim to the far bank and scramble clear. But the palomino had chosen a stretch which had once been a raised ford, and the water level here was no more than four feet.

'Oh no,' gasped Connie as the horse's front legs disappeared into the water, and collapsed under her. We watched helplessly as she thrashed around on her side trying to find some form of foothold, but the more she struggled, the worse her plight became.

As we pulled up panting at the bank side, it was obvious the animal was in serious trouble.

'Oh God,' cried Connie, 'she's going to drown.'

I could see this was a distinct possibility. The horse's head was half in the water, and despite desperate attempts it just couldn't raise it. Big Tim, puffing and sweating came alongside.

It took only a second for him to take in the situation, and half scrambling, half slipping down the bank side, he waded waist deep towards the struggling animal.

'All right old girl, all right.'

His voice was soothing as he approached the thrashing beast. At the sound of it the horse paused in its struggles.

'That's my girl, steady now, steady.'

Tim continued to intone the words as he stroked the half submerged face. He needed help.

Connie turned to me.

'We'll need the fire brigade . . . and tell them they'll need a sling.'

'I'll do it,' said Harry, who started running towards the nearest phone box. Meanwhile Connie had slipped off her skirt, kicked off her shoes and before I could stop her, had entered the water and was wading with three of the travelling men towards Big Tim.

'Leg must have gone,' he shouted to them. He pointed to the halter floating on the surface. 'Grab 'old of that and try and keep her head out of water.'

The four of them tugged on the rope, and we watched as Tim ducked under the water. As Connie and her helpers tried to haul the animal's head up, he tried to slip his mammoth shoulders under her neck. Suddenly the animal began thrashing again, knocking one of the gypsies off balance and sending Tim flying backwards back under water.

Gasping for breath he surfaced and tried twice more without success. Then, filling his lungs once again, he went down for the fourth time.

Using a submerged rock for support, he pressed upwards, his immense shoulder strength forcing the palomino's neck above the surface, and as the others pulled on the halter, the animal gave one final thrust and hauled herself upright.

Big Tim surfaced like some huge dripping sea creature. 'Keep 'old of that halter, don't let her move,' he gasped.

In the distance we could hear the siren of the approaching fire engine, and as the men made for the river bank, Connie stayed with Tim and stroked the muzzle of the trembling animal.

The fire officers had obviously done this type of rescue before. Fastening a wide sling around the horse's girth they began winching it towards the opposite bank. As it struggled clear of the water it was obvious the right foreleg was hideously damaged.

I hurried across the bridge and handed Connie her shoes and skirt which she slipped over her soaking underwear. Taking off my jacket I placed it around her shoulders.

'The deal is, you report the news, not make it,' I smiled.

Her teeth were chattering, but she refused to move until

Alan Phillips the local vet, who had been quickly on the scene, had examined the horse.

He shook his head slowly. 'Tim, there's only one thing to be done,' he said quietly.

The big man didn't speak, he just nodded, and placing his huge hands either side of the horse's face, bent his head until his forehead rested on the palomino's white blaze and we heard him whisper, 'Sorry old girl.'

He walked away past Connie and me without a word.

It took me ten minutes to drive Connie back to the White Hart for a shower and a change of clothing. When she came down into the bar, Jim Slater handed her a large brandy.

'Get that down yer,' he instructed her. 'Mark here tells me you're a heroine.'

'It was dreadful Jim. That poor horse.'

I could see tears welling in her eyes.

'Come on,' I said. 'We still have a job to do.'

The brandy helped to regain her composure, and by the time we got back and joined Harry in the Blue Cat, she had almost recovered.

'Did the vet put her down?' she asked Harry.

'Yes. Nature's way of providing dog food, I suppose.'

'You are an insensitive sod,' Connie retorted.

'Well at least we've got our story for today,' he said leaning back on his chair. 'What about the nationals Mark, do you think you can sell it?'

I wasn't sure. It was a nice local drama, but not one likely to inspire the national news desks. 'Unless you've got some really outstanding pics of our Connie here in her knickers.'

'You wouldn't dare,' she flashed.

I turned to Connie. 'So, who pinched Tim's horse?'

'They had nerve, I'll give them that, no one would give a second thought to a horse being led around the common today.' She was obviously thinking on similar lines to me. 'It had to be someone who wanted to nobble it, they couldn't kidnap it, not today of all days.'

'So they turned her loose and set the dog on her. The accident was an added unforeseen bonus for them.'

'What will happen about the race now?' she asked.

'Ganton will have to use another horse. One thing's for sure, Ronnie Muir won't be a happy man.'

'How do you make that out?'

With the palomino out of it, he stands to lose a packet if those heavy bets he took at 8/1 on Tommy Boy come home to roost. He told me himself that one punter had placed £100 on it to win.'

'Eight hundred quid,' Harry whistled. 'Not a bad day's work.' Do you reckon someone's stitching our Ronnie up?'

I could see Connie was confused. 'Hang on,' she protested. 'The purse auction you told me about hasn't taken place yet. How can a bookie take bets on horses that might not be running?'

'It's called inside information,' I told her.

At four o'clock, the gypsies gathered around Big Tim's caravan. Normally, with the exception of of Ronnie Muir, who was given special dispensation, no outsider was allowed to penetrate this hallowed circle, but thanks to Connie's brave effort in trying to rescue Tim's mare the three of us were allowed to witness the purse auction. We received some dark looks from the assembled fraternity, and Harry's camera was viewed with deep suspicion.

Ronnie Muir, looking worried, fidgeted uncomfortably next to me. But his inside information proved to be spot on. Harry Brewer laid down the challenge with a purse of £15. Seven others took it up, including Ganton, who announced that he would be riding a horse called Pebble. Brewer raised the purse to £50, then £75, before one of the gypsies withdrew. The six remaining matched each other pound for pound until Brewer finally raised the purse to £200, and as Ronnie had forecast, this left Tommy Boy to do battle with Harry Brewer and Ganton. Big Tim raised his hand for silence, and announced that the race would be run in Quarry Lane, a quiet stretch of highway leading to the hills.

Ronnie opened his book officially and money began changing hands rapidly. His earlier odds had taken a tumble, Ganton was now the outsider at 7/1 with Harry Brewer the 2/1-on favourite and Tommy Boy down to 2/1 against.

The *Weekly Times*, always gave good coverage to the fair, and in recent years, whilst not actually condoning the illegal race, always managed to publish a picture of the winner. So it was important for Harry to position himself at the winning post, and he set off with the advance party of gypsies whose job was to mark out the course and close the road with their wagons.

Big Tim grabbed Connie's arm. 'Now lass, you can do us another favour.' He handed her his scarlet neckerchief. 'I want 'yer to start the race for us.'

She gave me an embarrassed laugh. 'Will I be committing an offence?'

'Only if you manage a false start,' I chuckled.

We climbed onto Tim's flat cart and with scores of gypsies following on foot, Tim flicked the reins at the horse between the shafts and we set off for Quarry Lane.

Harry Brewer was a small dark man with a pinched face who looked as if he hadn't washed for a year. His pencil moustache and his restless dark eyes suggested a man with whom you would not care to do business. He was certainly not a man to cross.

'He looks a right villain,' Connie whispered to me, as we stood on the grass verge in the lane waiting for the riders to mount.

The slim piebald he was holding onto pawed the ground impatiently. Next to him was the sallow faced Tommy Boy, a youth with a shock of black curly hair who couldn't keep his eyes off Connie. His pony, the colour of sandpaper, constantly nodded its head, as if sharing some secret agreement with Ganton's mount Pebble, standing quietly alongside. Ganton, whose weatherbeaten face was a study in concentration, stood in front of his horse, holding her by the bridle.

Tim's chosen course wasn't a straight measured mile, but one that curved after about two hundred yards. By straining our necks we could actually see the finishing line in the distance to our right, and either side of the hedgerows lining the route, scores of spectators were now jostling for the best viewing positions. One of the travellers free-wheeled down the lane towards us on a rusty old bike and reported to Big Tim that the course was ready. At his signal the three riders made athletic leaps onto the bare backs of their mounts, and Connie, standing to one side on the verge, raised Big Tim's neckerchief.

It wasn't exactly a racing start, more an inspired trot, then the riders began hammering their heels into the horse's flanks and the race started in earnest. As they disappeared round the curve, I made Ganton the leader by about a length.

It was at that moment that Big Tim gave a loud groan and collapsed to the ground. At first I thought he had stumbled and fallen, but as he lay there, grey and unconscious, it was clear he needed urgent medical help.

Meanwhile a cry went up from the crowd watching the race. 'Brewer's,' I heard a gypsy shout.

But the race had now taken a back seat in our thoughts. It was essential we got Big Tim to hospital. Grabbing the old bike that had been left at the roadside, and leaving Connie to do what she could to comfort the gypsy, I pedalled back to the telephone box near the common and dialled for an ambulance.

By the time I rejoined Connie and the large gathering of onlookers, Ganton and the two ambulance men were bending over his stricken father. Turning an anxious face he asked them 'will he be all right?'

'Best get him to hospital quick, son,' said one of them.

Between them, they struggled to get Tim onto the stretcher and into the ambulance, with Ganton clambering in behind.

'What's the score?' I asked the driver.

Ignoring the question he slammed the door and ran to

the front and started the engine, and with siren blaring, the ambulance picked its way through the parting crowds.

'It's turning out to be quite a day,' said Harry, reloading his camera.

'Who won the race?' I asked him.

'Tommy Boy, by four lengths. Harry Brewer came off and Ganton was well beaten.

An hour later when I rang Jill at the hospital she confirmed that Big Tim was dead on arrival. She transferred me to the hospital spokesman who said it appeared Tim had died from a massive heart attack, but we would have to wait for the post-mortem.

As the news spread around Sessington, the travellers and gypsies began assembling in noisy groups. No longer was the common embraced in a festive atmosphere; the mood was now sombre, with an underlying feeling of tension, and as the day wore on there was a noticeable increase in the amount of drunkenness. This in itself might have ben contained, had it not been for the arrival in the main street of about twenty chanting thugs, led by Barry Chapel, a Dobermann at his heels.

Dressed in their black leather jackets, they were chanting threats and the words 'Kill the filthy gypsies' were clearly audible as they headed for the Blue Cat. They were in the bar before Dave Challenor realised what was happening.

Later he told us how a glass of beer had been spilled, followed by a scuffle, and within minutes the pub was the scene of a full blown riot. Chapel's men had armed themselves with all manner of weapons, knives, bicycle chains, brass knuckledusters, and home-made coshes. Taken by surprise and mostly the worse for drink, the gypsies didn't stand a chance, and when Chapel and his hooligans emerged into the street, laughing and cheering, and punching the air in victory, Dave's call to the Bridge-field police was academic.

It was like a battlefield when we got there. Two men were out cold on the floor, several had been cut about the face, and one man was clearly in agony as he nursed a badly shattered arm. Amongst the upturned tables and chairs, broken bottles and shattered glass littered the floor.

Harry started taking snatch pictures until I grabbed him by the shoulder.

'Harry, let's get out of here.'

Back in the street we watched in disbelief as the common was transformed into a battle zone, with running fights taking place amongst the startled horses. Chapel was in the thick of things, taking on all comers. Most of the visitors had fled to their cars, and those who did stay watched from a safe distance. When the police arrived their presence only served to inflame matters, and at one time it was difficult to make out just who was fighting whom. Finally after about half an hour they had the situation under control, and at least a dozen arrests had been made.

'We're going to have a busy time in court tomorrow morning,' I said to Connie.

We filed the riot story with the *Clarion* and sent a few paragraphs on spec to the nationals. Two of the tabloids were prepared to consider the horse rescue story, but only if Harry's pics were good enough. After supper we went over to the White Hart with Connie and drowned the memories of the day in Jim Slater's best bitter.

I covered the court alone the following morning, Connie having accepted the offer of a day off with gratitude. The presiding magistrate was Polly Stenhouse, who tended to take a liberal view of these sort of punch-ups, and fined the lot of them £25 each and bound them over to keep the peace.

One name was missing from the charge sheet.

'Where's Chapel?' I whispered to the young police constable standing behind the press bench.

'I gather he legged it before our lot could grab him,' was the doleful reply.

Wednesday's post-mortem on Big Tim confirmed the hospital's first opinion and returned a verdict of death by natural causes,

probably induced by the strain and stress trying to save his
beloved horse.

That night I received a telephone call from Ganton. 'You
are the writer fella that called the ambulance for Da aren't you?
Da would have wanted to thank you.'

'I'm sorry about your father, and his horse,' I replied lamely.

'Not to fret. It's all been taken care of. Funeral's on Friday.
It would be nice if you would put a bit about him in t'paper.'

'Where's the service being held?'

'Bridgefield cemetery, in the Romany corner, Revd Blake
will bury him, but procession will start from High Green.'

'OK, I'll get my assistant to come and see you, we'll need
some background on your father.'

'A spunky young lass that, not many would have gone in
'watter like she did. Any help you want, just seek me out, and
thanks again for trying to help Da.'

Since the Emma Proudfoot business, there had been a certain
reserve between the Revd Blake and me, but he sounded
cheerful enough when I phoned him to mark my card on a
Romany funeral. 'As a matter of fact I've never officiated at
one, but I understand they can be quite lavish affairs. They
want the service to be held outside in the cemetery.'

'It will have to be some grave to take Big Tim's coffin,' I
suggested.

'Yes, and we haven't got an official grave digger, he's down
with a bad back, but fortunately the gypsies have offered to
take care of things.'

Bridgefield high street was bustling that Friday morning, and
as Connie and I arrived at the High Green we were staggered
to see scores of mourners assembling. I knew Big Tim was well
thought of, but there were travelling families here from all over
the country. Ganton appeared to be the chief organiser, and
we watched him in this dark overcoat, a white scarf at his
throat, talking in turn to groups of similarly dressed men.

The womenfolk, keeping a watchful eye on bright-eyed
children, wore black scarves over their heads.

But it was the flowers that caught everybody's attention. I had never seen so many floral tributes at a funeral. To carry them all, three horse-drawn flat carts were required. A fourth cart carried the huge walnut coffin, a polished shrine set amidst a carpet of white lilies and heart shaped posies, and topped with a large cross fashioned from red roses.

Connie told me that Mary Livingstone, who owned the only flower shop in the town, had been unable to cope with the number of orders, and had called in help from florists as far as thirty miles away.

Ganton began arranging the cortége, one flower cart ahead of the coffin, the other two at the rear. The horses, each wearing a plume of mauve feathers, pawed the ground impatiently as the mourners took their positions at the rear, many carrying more wreaths and bunches of flowers.

Ahead of the leading horse was Charlie Bell, from the Bridgefield Brass Band, who was strapped to an enormous bass drum. Suddenly from the assembled throng, Ganton appeared with a small frail woman wearing a black veil covering her head and face.

'Who's the woman,' I asked a panting Harry who had found difficulty in finding a parking place.

'It's Ganton's mother,' said Connie. 'He introduced me to her the other day.'

At Ganton's signal, Charlie Bell struck his drum with such force that Connie standing beside me almost jumped into the air. The lead horse didn't like it much either, and the man standing alongside holding the rein, had to struggle to keep control of the startled beast. The drum was a signal for every man in the procession to remove his hat, and to the doleful beat of Charlie's drum, Big Tim started his last journey through Bridgefield. Forewarned of the size of the funeral, the police had sealed off the high street to traffic, which was just as well because Harry and I estimated there were over 400 travellers filing behind their late leader.

The dignity of the occasion was shattered when the procession reached a point opposite the post office. Although Barry Chapel was nowhere to be seen, it didn't take a genius to guess that the yobs chanting their obscene insults were the same as those who had caused the riots in Sessington earlier in the week.

'Someone is going to pay for that,' I said to Harry.

But to their credit not one of the mourners broke ranks to silence their tormentors.

We hurried ahead and waited for the procession at the cemetery, where the Revd John Blake, in cassock and surplice, was waiting at the graveside, flanked by half a dozen hefty travelling men. The spoil from the newly dug grave was masked with more flowers, and the floor of the grave was a carpet of lilies. The six men lifted Big Tim from the cart and gently lowered him into the thick cushion of blooms. The flowers around the grave were then placed on top of the coffin and John Blake started the simple service. He referred to Tim as the paterfamilias of the gypsies, the man who had looked after their interests, settled their arguments, and brought dignity to their cause.

At the end, Tim's weeping widow came forward with Ganton and they added their own wreaths. Silently they moved away, and only then did the rest of the mourners come forward in orderly fashion and file past Big Tim's grave. By the time they had left, the area was almost knee deep in flowers.

Harry completed his picture coverage, and we too departed, leaving the six gypsies to start filling in the grave.

'That was quite something,' said Connie as we grabbed a sandwich and a beer in the Three Jugs. 'I'm really going to miss all this.'

'I was surprised our friend Barry Chapel didn't put in an appearance,' said Harry. 'Not like him to miss an opportunity to cause trouble. Anyway, I must dash. Will I see you before you go, Connie?'

'I doubt it Harry. I start with the *Clarion* on Monday.' She looked at both of us tenderly and smiled.

'Well, I'll see you around,' said Harry.

Connie threw her arms around him and gave him a hug. 'Take care.'

After he had gone I bought another round of drinks, and felt in my pocket for the gift Jill and I had bought her.

'Oh Mark, you shouldn't.'

'I know. I told Jill you weren't worth it, but she insisted.'

She put her tongue out at me, then slipped her arms around my neck and kissed me on the lips. 'I'm going to miss you a lot, Mark Devlin. Thanks for everything.'

'It's me who should be grateful. Thanks to your help, I can now afford to buy those little luxuries I've always hankered after. Socks, handkerchiefs, food, that sort of thing.'

She laughed again, opened the bottle of perfume, and kissed me on the cheek. 'I've learned a hell of a lot working with you. Can we keep in touch?' Her voice was soft, and gentle.

'Don't worry, I'll be asking Paul Winter for progress reports. Come on, drink up, you've still got to file copy.'

Like Jill, I'd enjoyed having Connie around, and now she was back with the *Clarion*, I had to revert to doing things for myself, like the daily chore of checking with the emergency services to see if they had anything worthwhile to report.

'You look very serious. Anything wrong?' Jill asked, after I had made such a call to Bridgefield police.

'Barry Chapel,' I replied, putting the phone down. 'He's never been seen since the horse fair fracas last week. It looks as if he doesn't intend coming back.'

'Good riddance. What makes them think that?'

'His long-suffering next door neighbour reported a disgusting smell coming from Chapel's back yard this morning, and when they checked, they found Chapel's Rottweiler dog. It had been there some while, its throat was cut.'

'Oh, how horrible.'

'The police think he's left the area and the dog was an encumberance, so he simply got rid of it.'

I might have not given this incident a second thought had it not been for the conversation I had the following day, with Edith Perth, at the Sessington parish council meeting. As usual, she was seeing to the fire, before the councillors arrived, and it was while we were discussing the horse fair riots that she told me about the fight she had witnessed from her cottage window that night.

Evidently she had see an old van pull up and three men jump out and grab this chap on the pavement. 'They just about beat him senseless, and then bundled him in the back of the van and drove off,' she said.

'Did you recognise them?'

'No it was too dark. I phoned the police, but I don't know if they did anything about it.'

The main item on the council agenda that night was Sessington Fair. Sean Kelly and Harry Jenkins proposed that the Fair should be banned in future, but John Briggs argued that such a move would only be giving in to the hooligans, and after a fierce debate he won the day by one vote.

After the meeting, I called in at the Blue Cat, which had almost been restored to normal, following the fracas on horse fair day. Over a pint at the bar, I told Dave Challenor what the council had decided.

He nodded agreement. 'This was the first time there has been any trouble in this pub on fair day since I came here twelve years ago, and from what I overheard the other night, Barry Chapel and his mates had best look out. The gypsies have a few scores to settle.'

The following morning on my way to Bridgefield, my route took me past the cemetery. Over in the Romany corner, a stonemason was erecting a headstone over Big Tim's grave. Intrigued to see what the inscription was, I pulled up and walked over. The gold lettering on the black marble was short and to the point.

'In loving memory of Tim the Gypsy, 1900–1970', and at the foot, 'Goodness above all evil'.

Back in the car I jotted down the inscription in my notebook and then parking my car in the high street, I crossed over to the court room to spend an unproductive morning listening to a series of dull, inconsequential cases. By lunch-time I was ready for a pint in the Three Jugs, where the conversation inevitably got round to Big Tim and the riots.

'Gypsies will miss t'big fella,' said Bobby Watson, pulling a couple of pints. 'He was a good man, not like that evil bastard Chapel.'

I thought of Tim's epitaph I had seen earlier, and once again the words 'goodness' and 'evil' sprang to mind.

Finishing my beer, I walked towards the car, but on impulse I turned and crossed over to the police station.

'Are you out of your mind?' exploded Insp. Yarrum, after I had been shown into his office and said my piece. 'You want us to dig up a corpse because you have a hunch there might be two bodies in the coffin?'

'A mighty big coffin,' I persisted. 'And Chapel has gone missing. Look, all I'm saying is the gypsies had a few good reasons to get rid of him.'

'Let's hear them,' said Yarrum.

'For starters there's the stabbing of one of their clan last year, and the riots stirred up by Chapel and his mob last week. It's odds on that it was Chapel's Rottweiler that chased Tim's horse to its death which in turn lead to the death of Tim himself. Ronnie Muir told me he'd lost a packet on the race, which he claimed had been rigged by Chapel's mob. Then there's the beating and a possible abduction witnessed by Edith Perth, the slaughter of Chapel's dog, and now the inscription.'

'What inscription?'

I told him what I had just seen on Tim's headstone. 'Goodness above all evil'.

He sat back, deep in thought.

'Look, I thought you might be interested, that's all,' I said getting up.

As I reached the door he mumbled, 'Do you know the hassle

we would have to go through with the coroner to get an exhumation order?'

'Not my problem,' I said, closing the door.

Whatever it took to get that order, it didn't take very long. The following day Yarrum rang me. 'If we don't find anything, there's no story. Is that a deal?'

'Yes. If Chapel isn't there, you can put Big Tim back, and as far as I'm concerned I won't publish a word about it.'

The exhumation took place in the early hours of the following morning. Dawn hadn't broken when the police contingent drew up in two unmarked cars, parked well away from the cemetery, and put screens around the grave. It took four of them two hours before their spades unearthed the massive coffin, and a further half hour to raise it to the surface.

'God, what a stench,' complained a young constable. I grabbed a handkerchief and jammed it over my nose.

'Come on, get a move on,' urged Yarrum, conscious of the sun beginning to rise above the distant hills.

Minutes later, they had unfastened the brass wing-nuts and we were staring into the decomposing face of Big Tim. The main reason for the size of the coffin was the amount of Romany memorabilia it had to accommodate, including bits of the palomino's harness, and twelve large cushions, all delicately hand embroidered with scenes of a traveller's life.

Yarrum, looked at me scornfully. 'Just remember our deal,' he said threateningly. 'No body . . .'

He was interrupted by a shout from an officer prodding around inside the grave. 'Gov. Over here.'

At the funeral I had felt there was something rather odd about the carpet of lilies on the floor of the grave. Crushing them with the heavy coffin seemed such a dreadful waste of good blooms. Now as the constable began forking them out, he knew where the stench of decomposing flesh was coming from.

Chapel was lying face down, and it didn't need a forensic scientist to tell us he'd been stabbed to death.

'I owe you one, Mark,' said Yarrum quietly.

My coverage made front page news in almost every national newspaper, and three of the tabloids carried double page spreads alongside Harry's dramatic horse fair pics.

The following morning Connie rang with her congratulations. 'You are a rotten bastard,' she laughed. 'Getting rid of me, so you can have all the action. Who do you reckon did it, then?'

'Well, they brought Ganton in to help with their enquiries, but they couldn't hold him, they had no evidence to link him with Chapel's death. The rest of the travellers who were at the fair are now dispersed all over the county, and anyway, who is to say it was one of them, Chapel had so many enemies. I reckon it will go down as one of Sessington's unsolved mysteries and in years to come, it will be all part of the local folklore. It'll certainly be the talking point in the White Hart for the next few months, that's for sure.'

'Speaking of talking points,' she cut in. 'Have you heard our news, about Paul Winter?'

'What's he been up to now?'

'He's just gone and landed the managing director's job. He's taking over from Kevin Johnson, who took Sir John's advice and resigned.'

'Well done Paul.'

'Yes,' she enthused. 'That means we'll be getting a new editor. Who do you suppose will get the job?'

'Don't ask me,' I laughed. 'I'm only the District Man.'